MEN
in
UNIFORM

Courteous, courageous and commanding—
these heroes lay it all on the line for the
people they love in more than fifty stories about
loyalty, bravery and romance.
Don't miss a single one!

AMANDA STEVENS

THE HERO'S SON

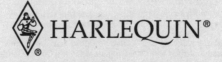

TORONTO • NEW YORK • LONDON
AMSTERDAM • PARIS • SYDNEY • HAMBURG
STOCKHOLM • ATHENS • TOKYO • MILAN • MADRID
PRAGUE • WARSAW • BUDAPEST • AUCKLAND

Recycling programs
for this product may
not exist in your area.

ISBN-13: 978-0-373-36292-9

THE HERO'S SON

AMANDA STEVENS

is a bestselling author of more than thirty novels of romantic suspense. In addition to being a Romance Writers of America RITA® Award finalist, she is also a recipient of awards for Career Achievement in Romantic Mystery and Career Achievement in Romantic Suspense from *RT Book Reviews* magazine. She currently resides in Texas. To find out more about past, present and future projects, please visit her website at www.amandastevens.com.

This book is dedicated to my editor, Huntley Fitzpatrick.

PROLOGUE

THE BANGING ON THE front door awakened five-year-old Violet from a deep sleep. Frightened, she called out. Mommy and Daddy were in the next room, watching TV. Why didn't they come?

Her heart pounding, Violet got out of bed and crept to her bedroom door. Mommy and Daddy were standing in the living room, and for a moment, Violet felt safe. Then she saw their faces. They looked the way she felt when she'd had a really bad dream. Or seen something scary on TV. But mommies and daddies weren't supposed to get scared, were they?

The banging at the door sounded again, and someone shouted, "Police! Open up!"

Mommy grabbed Daddy's arm. "Cletus, my God, what's going on?"

Daddy's face was white. He looked sick. "I don't know. I'd better let them in."

But before he could open the door, it burst open, shattering the wood frame. Mommy screamed as three men rushed in and grabbed Daddy. "Don't move," one of the men said. "Or we'll blow your head off."

Hiding behind her bedroom door, Violet shoved a fist against her mouth to keep from crying. She'd never been so scared. Mommy had always told her if she were ever lost or in trouble to look for a policeman. He would

help her. But these men didn't have on uniforms, like
Mommy had shown her, and they didn't have the pretty
shiny badges that Violet liked so much, either. All they
had were guns. And Violet knew guns were bad. Very
bad.

All three of the men were scary, but it was the big
man with the dark hair that frightened Violet the most.
She'd learned about the devil in Sunday-school class,
had even seen a picture of him in a book, and that was
who she thought of now. The big man didn't have horns
or a tail, but her Sunday-school teacher had said the
devil could disguise himself in many ways. Even as a
policeman.

Help us, Violet prayed. *Please help us.*

The television Mommy and Daddy had been watching was still on, and Violet could hear bits of a news
broadcast, something about the little boy who had been
kidnapped. His picture was all over the news. Violet
saw it every time she turned on the TV to watch her
favorite shows. She didn't want to think about what was
happening, how scared she was, so she tried instead to
remember the kidnapped boy's name.

And then she heard someone say it. Adam Kingsley.
Yes, that was it. Adam Kingsley had been kidnapped
from his bedroom, and no one knew where he was or
what had happened to him. Mommy said everyone in
Memphis was looking for him.

Violet had been so frightened when she first heard
about the kidnapping. What if someone kidnapped *her?*
She could think of nothing scarier than to be taken from
her mommy and daddy, but then Mommy had told her
that Adam Kingsley had been kidnapped because his
parents were rich. His father was an important man.

Violet had nothing to worry about. Her daddy was just an out-of-work auto mechanic.

Violet heard Adam Kingsley's name again, and she thought it must be coming from the TV. Then she realized the big man was saying the little boy's name. Saying it over and over as he grabbed Daddy and shouted, "Where is he? Where is he, you piece of scum?"

Daddy's hands were fastened behind his back, like Violet had seen policemen on TV do to bad men. The big man shoved Daddy, and he fell backward, hitting his head against the corner of the coffee table.

Blood ran from the cut on his head, and Mommy screamed. She tried to run to him, but the big man pushed her away. She fell, too, and Violet's heart began to pound, not just in fear, but because she was angry. She ran out of her room as fast as she could.

"Don't hurt my mommy!" she screamed. "Don't you hurt my mommy!"

She tried to grab the big man's arm, but he just pushed her away and turned back to Daddy, who had been pulled to his feet by the other two men.

Blood ran down Daddy's face as he looked at Violet and Mommy. "I'm innocent, Grace. You have to believe me. They're setting me up—"

"Shut up!" the big man yelled.

The men dragged Daddy across the room. One of them opened the front door, and for the first time, Violet realized there was a crowd outside. The tiny front yard was filled with people, and in the street, lights flashed on top of police cars.

Mommy got up off the floor and ran outside. Violet didn't know what else to do but follow. But there was so much noise outside. So many people. Violet started to cry. She saw some of their neighbors in the front yard, and they were shouting bad words at Daddy. A bottle shattered against the house, and Mommy began to cry, too.

Violet tried to run to Daddy, but the big man caught her. He knelt and looked into her eyes. Violet began to shake, she was so scared. What if he really was the devil, come to take her to hell?

He reached out for her, and Violet tried to pull away. Somewhere near them, a bright light flashed in her face, and she blinked. She heard an excited voice yell, "Did you get that shot?"

The big man patted her head. In a soft voice, he told her everything would be all right. But his eyes—eyes that looked like the picture in the Sunday-school book— told her something else, and Violet backed away from him, away from his touch.

Another man came up beside him. He was dressed in a uniform like Mommy had shown her, and Violet thought he would make the big man go away. That he would help her. But instead, he said, "We found part of the ransom money in the trunk of his car. Just where you said it would be, Sergeant Colter."

The big man stood and walked away from Violet, but the fear didn't leave her. She knew who he was now, and she knew she would never forget him for as long as she lived.

The devil's name was Sergeant Colter.

CHAPTER ONE

*THIRTY-ONE YEARS LATER...*Sergeant Brant Colter caught sight of the tall brunette in the crowd ahead and quickened his steps, trying not to lose her. Another woman, a petite blonde, walked beside her, but Brant had no interest in her. It was the dark-haired woman he wanted.

He knew very little about her, except that her name was Valerie Snow, she worked as an investigative reporter for the *Memphis Journal,* and she seemed hellbent on destroying Brant's family.

He grimaced, thinking about the article that had appeared in the *Journal* yesterday. According to Valerie Snow, the wrong man had been sent to prison thirty-one years ago for little Adam Kingsley's kidnapping and murder, a crime that was almost as famous as the Lindbergh case.

She claimed that the three detectives who had made the arrest—Judd Colter, Raymond Colter and Hugh Rawlins—had planted evidence to frame Cletus Brown and had then suppressed witnesses who could have cleared him.

In short, Valerie Snow alleged that one or all of them had concocted an elaborate conspiracy comparable only to the Kennedy assassination, and all because of their pride; their "hubris," she called it. They had been humiliated by the press and by the FBI, and were desperate for an arrest. Desperate to become heroes.

And they *had* become heroes, Brant thought. The three of them were almost legendary in the department— his father, his uncle and his mentor. The three men who had probably influenced Brant's life the most.

But it wasn't just Valerie Snow's outlandish accusations that were so troublesome. The timing of the article couldn't have been worse. Brant's father was recovering from a stroke; Raymond's son, Austin, had just announced his intention of running for Congress; and Hugh Rawlins, the only one of the three still on the police force, was retiring in another month with full honors and benefits. The last thing any of them needed was to have their names dragged through the mud by some reporter out to make a name for herself.

The two women stopped in front of an expensive boutique and stared at the window display. Brant stepped into a shoe store next door, not wanting to take a chance on being spotted. It was cool inside, and he stood for a moment, enjoying the respite from the sultry humidity.

A middle-aged clerk wearing a bad toupee sauntered up to him. "May I help you?"

"Just browsing," Brant muttered, waving the man away.

From his vantage point inside the store, Brant could see Valerie Snow clearly. She was still looking at the window display as she chatted with her companion, and Brant took the opportunity to study her.

She wasn't at all what he'd expected. After reading her article, he'd pictured her as a militant-looking woman with combat boots and chopped-off hair, but she was nothing like that. Tall and thin, with the toned body of a runner, she had legs that went on forever and long, dark hair that shone like polished ebony in the late-afternoon sunlight.

Even standing still, she looked restless. Energy seemed to radiate from her lithe body, making Brant wonder what her temper might be like. She wore a dark blue suit with a fitted jacket and a short, slim skirt. Her nails were unpainted, as was her mouth, but he figured the latter was because she'd chewed off all her lipstick and hadn't had the patience to freshen it.

By comparison, the woman beside her looked cool and serene in a yellow sundress that reminded Brant of a frosted glass of lemonade. Her unhurried movements were that of a true Southern belle. She was the type of woman Brant had always been attracted to, but it was Valerie Snow who drew his gaze now. Valerie Snow who held his undivided attention.

Brant wasn't sure what his original intention had been when he'd followed her from the *Journal*'s offices. He supposed at some point he would catch up with her, introduce himself, and ask her what the hell she thought she was doing.

Not in an official capacity, of course. She hadn't broken any laws that he was aware of, but still…. He'd always been of the mind that it was wise to seek out your enemies. Get to know them. Find out *their* weaknesses.

She left her friend at the boutique and started down the street alone. Brant exited the shoe store and fell in behind her. The five o'clock pedestrian traffic was heavy, with people streaming out of the downtown office buildings in a hurry to get home.

As they rounded a corner, Brant almost lost her in the crowd, but then he caught sight of her dark hair in the group of people standing at the intersection, waiting for the light to change. He hung back, not wanting to get too close. But as if sensing his scrutiny, she turned her head, her eyes scouring the crowd, and Brant thought for a moment she'd spotted him. Then she turned and faced the street again.

More and more people joined the throng waiting at the light. Valerie was up front, near the street. Brant kept his eyes fastened on her, but his peripheral vision caught a movement in the crowd. His gaze shifted, and for just a split second, he thought he saw a familiar face—an informant his father had once used. A man who would sell his mother's soul for a quick buck.

Remy Devereaux had disappeared a long time ago, and if he was still alive, which Brant seriously doubted, he would be getting on in years. He wasn't likely to still be out hustling in the streets.

But if he was, what the hell kind of coincidence had brought him here, to the very street corner where Valerie Snow stood waiting for the light to change?

A bus lumbered down the street, and the crowd automatically stepped back from the curb. Brant lost sight of the man, and when he tried to spot Valerie Snow, he realized he'd lost her, too.

And then someone screamed.

Brant reacted instantly. As he leaped forward, the mass of people seemed to part, and he caught a quick glimpse of dark hair and blue fabric. She lay sprawled on the street, directly in front of the oncoming bus.

With a spurt of adrenaline, Brant lunged forward

again. But the crowd, which had parted a second earlier, now closed in on him. He couldn't move.

"Police!" he shouted, flashing his badge. "Move back!"

Everyone did as they were told, but by the time Brant made his way through to the street, the bus had sped by. Someone screamed again, and with a sick feeling in the pit of his stomach, Brant gazed down at Valerie Snow's crumpled body.

Someone had pulled her out of the way in the nick of time. She lay on her back on the sidewalk, her eyes closed, her hair fanned about her face like a dark halo.

He didn't think she was dead, but he had no idea how badly she might be hurt. Flashing his badge again to ward off the crowd, he knelt beside her and felt for a pulse.

"Is she going to be all right?" a woman asked anxiously.

Instead of answering her, Brant said, "Call 911. We need an ambulance."

"Oh, God, is she—"

"Just make the call. Now!"

The woman's face paled, and her hands trembled as she opened her purse and pulled out a cell phone.

Brant heard someone in the crowd say, "Man, did you see what happened? She just jumped in front of that bus! Must have a death wish or something."

The stunned rumblings went on and on, but Brant tuned them out. He turned his attention to the woman lying on the sidewalk, so still and silent. A sprinkling of freckles across her nose stood out starkly against her pale skin.

She should have looked vulnerable, but didn't. Somehow, even in repose, she managed to appear strong and intelligent. A woman perfectly capable of pissing off some pretty powerful people in this town.

She stirred and moaned.

"Take it easy," Brant said. "The ambulance is on its way."

Her lids fluttered, and then her eyes opened. They were gray, the color of rain clouds.

"What happened?" She tried to sit up, but Brant pushed her gently back to the street.

"You were almost hit by a bus," someone in the crowd told her.

For the first time, she trained her gaze on Brant, and her eyes widened in shock. Or was it fear? Her lips moved frantically, but Brant couldn't understand what she was saying. He leaned closer to her and got a whiff of an expensive perfume, something as deep and sultry as a hot Southern night.

She tried to shrink away from him. "It's okay," Brant said gently. "I'm not going to hurt you. You fell in front of a bus, but someone pulled you out of the way in time. You'll be fine."

She shook her head and mouthed, "No." She trembled all over, and for a moment, Brant thought she must have gone into shock.

"You'll be fine," he repeated, whipping off his sport coat to spread over her. "Just hang in there."

"I didn't fall," she whispered, shaking uncontrollably.

"What?"

Her gaze locked onto his. Fear deepened in her gray eyes. "I didn't fall," she said. "I was pushed."

VALERIE SAT ON THE BED in the emergency room at Mercy General Hospital and tried to corral her racing thoughts.

No way could he have been the same man.

No way could he have remained unchanged after thirty-one years.

And yet she'd seen him with her own eyes!

Her heart had almost stopped when she'd looked up into those black eyes. Eyes just as cold and dark as the ones she remembered.

"Devil eyes," she'd always called them.

She shivered, just thinking about him. "I have to get out of here."

"What's your hurry?" Dr. Allen asked her. He was a young, good-looking resident who wore faded jeans and scuffed Nikes and made Valerie feel about a hundred and two. "You just got here."

"I don't like hospitals," she muttered.

He looked down at her with a wounded look. "I'm hurt. Truly hurt by that remark."

"Nothing personal." She'd been trying to ignore his flirting ever since she'd been brought in, but it wasn't easy. Dr. Allen was nothing if not charming.

"So what's the verdict?" she asked wearily.

"A few cuts and bruises. You're going to be pretty sore for a few days. I'm still waiting to have a look at your X rays, but I don't expect to find any broken bones. You're one lucky young lady, from everything I've heard."

Valerie supposed it wasn't every day one got pushed in front of a city bus and survived. If she closed her eyes, she could still feel herself pitching forward into the street, could still feel that moment of terror when she'd looked up to see the bus racing toward her like some huge steel monster. She could actually feel the heat from its engine, like the hot breath of death.

She put a quivering hand to her forehead. She had to get out of here. Find out what was going on.

Find out who wanted to kill her.

"Look, I'm perfectly fine," she insisted. "Good as new. And I really do have to be going. There's a press conference I have to get to." She tried to hop down from the bed, but every bone in her body screamed in protest. She groaned and offered only a token struggle when the doctor eased her back down. "I can't stay here," she whispered, as a wave of dizziness swept over her.

Dr. Allen said sternly, "I'm afraid the press conference will just have to wait. At least until I get those X rays."

"How long?"

"We're a little short-staffed this afternoon. Could take a while."

Valerie suppressed another groan. The antiseptic smell of the hospital made her nauseous, and for a moment, she thought she might actually pass out. Not just from the scent, but from the memories. She hadn't been in a hospital since those long, lonely nights six weeks ago, when she'd kept vigil over her mother, waiting for her to die.

Dr. Allen patted her hand. "Don't worry. I'll get you sprung as soon as I can. In the meantime, try to enjoy our hospitality. I've given you a mild painkiller to make you a little more comfortable. Relax and let the medication take effect. Doctor's orders. You look as if you could use a little downtime."

Downtime? Valerie wasn't even sure she remembered

what that was. She'd been operating on nervous energy and caffeine for so long, she was afraid to stop, afraid that if she did, she might never get going again.

But in spite of her determination to get out of there as quickly as possible, the medication made her feel a bit woozy, and she knew there was no way she could get herself home, let alone to Austin Colter's press conference.

Maybe I should call Julian, she thought, but even that task seemed too great.

Besides, she didn't feel like dealing with her boss at the moment. He would be more interested in getting a good story than in her welfare, and Valerie wasn't up to any questions. She first wanted to sort out what had happened for herself, but she couldn't seem to stay focused. Her mind began to drift as the drug took effect, and suddenly she was back in the little house in a Chicago suburb where she'd grown up, going through her mother's personal belongings the day after the funeral.

Valerie had wanted to get the painful job over with as quickly as possible. But that afternoon, she'd found more than just possessions in her mother's house. More than just memories. She'd found a truth so devastating, her life had been changed forever.

For over thirty years, Valerie had believed her father guilty of the heinous crime for which he had been convicted. Why else had she and her mother been called such vile and vicious names after her father's arrest? Why else had their home been targeted for terrorism? And more important, why else had she and her mother fled town in the middle of the night? Why had her mother changed their names, hidden their true identities, if not to escape the stigma of being the wife and daughter of a child-killer?

For over thirty years, Valerie had tried to hide from her past; from the shame and self-doubt that were almost consuming at times. She was the daughter of an infamous kidnapper who had taken the life of a child. What did that make *her?* Cletus Brown's blood ran in her veins. Was she like him in any way? Was she, herself, capable of violence?

For over thirty years, Valerie had never allowed herself to become close to anyone. She'd never had any friends to speak of, had never gotten involved in a serious relationship. She'd told herself it was because she was too busy building a career, but deep down, she'd always known it was because she was afraid that the terrible names people had called her in the past—the awful things they'd screamed at her when her father had been arrested—were true. That she was tainted, the offspring of a monster.

Only in her dreams had her father remained an innocent man. Only in her dreams was the real villain the man with the cold, black eyes. A man Valerie had never been able to forget.

For over thirty years, Sergeant Colter had haunted her sleep.

But it wasn't until after her mother's death, when Valerie had found her mother's diary hidden away among a cache of newspaper clippings and books about the Kingsley kidnapping, along with mementos from their former life, that Valerie had finally understood why she'd never been able to forget Sergeant Colter.

Her instincts about him had been right. He was an evil man who had set her father up. He'd made her father take the fall for a crime he hadn't committed. Cletus Brown *was* an innocent man.

Valerie's mother had gone to her grave still believing in him. They hadn't left Memphis because Grace Brown thought her husband guilty, but because she was afraid for her daughter's safety. There were men in Memphis, powerful men, who were willing to kill to keep Cletus Brown behind bars. To keep the truth from coming out.

And so Violet and Grace Brown had disappeared, and Cletus had gone silently to prison where he had remained for the past thirty-one years.

As Valerie had read her mother's diary that afternoon, it had become crystal clear to her what she must do. She would prove to the world that her father was innocent. She would free him from prison, and in so doing, free herself from the awful burden of guilt she had carried with her for almost her entire life.

The very next day, Valerie had quit her job at the *Chicago Sun-Times,* sent her résumé to the *Memphis Journal,* packed up a few of her belongings, along with her mother's diary and the box of mementos, and headed for Memphis, her birthplace, searching for truth, justice, and maybe, if she were honest with herself, a little revenge.

And now it's come to this, she thought, still trying to fight the hold the drug had on her.

She'd known from the first that the series of articles she'd planned about the Kingsley kidnapping wouldn't go over well with a lot of powerful people in this city. The reputations of three well-respected men were all at stake, and she'd known they wouldn't take her accusations lying down.

The Kingsley kidnapping had affected a lot of people, and when the truth finally came out, lives would be ruined.

But one life would be saved.

And that was the only one that could be allowed to matter, Valerie thought, as she closed her eyes and finally succumbed to the medication.

THE DREAM WAS ALWAYS the same. Her name was Violet again, and she was back in that tiny house in southeast Memphis, watching through the crack in her bedroom door. She heard her mother scream, saw her father collapse to the floor, and then the big man turned and looked at Violet. Looked at her with those cold, black eyes.

The devil's eyes.

Violet tried to scream, but no sound came out. She tried to shrink away, but couldn't move. She was trapped, mesmerized by a gaze so dark and evil, she felt herself sinking into those bottomless depths from which she knew there would be no escape.

But she had to try. She had to try and save herself. She had to try and save her father.

Because if she didn't, no one else would.

Violet fought her way up from the black pit. She struggled to free herself from the terror that claimed her, night after night.

As she finally reached the surface, the terror gave way to confusion, and Violet slowly became Valerie. But then she opened her eyes to find the devil himself staring down at her.

CHAPTER TWO

VALERIE GASPED and sprang up in bed.

"Take it easy. I didn't mean to startle you." His voice was deep and rich, not in the least threatening, but shivers scurried up Valerie's spine. He reached out to ease her back against the pillows, but Valerie shrank away from him. "I'm Sergeant Colter," he said.

What did one say to one's nightmare?

"Valerie Snow," she managed, clutching the sheet to her breast.

After her initial shock began to subside, Valerie realized who he must be. Why hadn't she thought of it earlier? He had to be Judd Colter's son because he was the spitting image of his father as he had looked thirty-one years ago when he'd stormed into a tiny home in southeast Memphis and changed three lives forever.

The resemblance almost took Valerie's breath away.

She found herself staring up at him, studying his face longer than she should have, trying to analyze him with a reporter's eye for detail.

There were subtle differences, she decided. He wasn't *exactly* like his father. At least, not physically.

He was just as tall, but leaner than Judd Colter had been. His hair was just as dark, but he didn't wear it in a military style like his father had. The thick strands brushed against his shirt collar, gleaming blue-black in the harsh fluorescent lighting.

His features were more even than his father's. *And more handsome,* Valerie thought, startled to feel the quiver of butterflies in her stomach.

Oh, yes, there were definitely differences, but one thing remained the same: his eyes were just as dark and just as cold as his father's.

Valerie shivered and tried to look away. "What do you want?"

"I need to talk to you."

Reluctantly she met his gaze. "What about?"

One dark brow rose in surprise. Or was it condescension? "You've made a pretty serious accusation, Ms. Snow. Or have you forgotten?"

At first, she thought he was talking about her article, then she realized he meant the incident with the bus. "You mean when I said someone tried to kill me?"

Something flashed in his dark eyes. Something Valerie couldn't quite define. "You didn't say that exactly. You said you were pushed."

She forced a harsh laugh. "Semantics, Sergeant Colter."

"Hardly. Even if you were pushed, it could have been an accident."

"Even *if?*" Valerie glared up at him. "I said I was pushed, and I was. And I think it was *very* deliberate."

He took out a pen and notebook and pulled up a chair. "Why don't we get the paperwork out of the way first, and then you can tell me what you think happened. What's your full name?" When she hesitated, he glanced up. "Is that question too difficult for you?"

There was enough arrogance in his voice to stir her

temper. *Yes, and you have no idea why,* she thought bitterly. "Is this going to take long?" Maybe if she stalled him, he would give up and go away. What was he going to do, anyway? Go looking for someone who had a reason to push her in front of a bus?

Well, he didn't have far to look, did he?

"That depends on you," he said.

She shrugged. "Guess I'm not going anywhere for a while." *That's it,* she thought. *Tough it out. Don't let him get to you.*

After all, she was good at pretending, wasn't she? She'd learned a long time ago not to let anyone see the real person, the real emotions, behind her hardened veneer.

"Your name," he repeated, his pen poised over his notebook. His hands were large and well shaped, Valerie noticed. And ringless. He wasn't married. She wondered why.

"Valerie Anne Snow."

He started scribbling. "Address?"

She rattled off her street address and he wrote it down.

"All right," he said, glancing up at her. "Why don't you tell me what happened?"

"Just the facts, ma'am. Right?" When he didn't respond to her sarcasm, Valerie shrugged and said, "Angie and I had just left work—"

"Angie?"

"Angela Casey. She writes an advice column for the *Journal.* That's where I work," she added, trying to gauge his reaction.

There was none. He appeared to be made of ice. "Go on."

"She was meeting someone for an early dinner, and so I left her on Front Street and headed for city hall, for Austin Colter's press conference. I wanted to get there early, before anyone else showed up—" She stopped short, wondering if that was why Sergeant Colter had arrived on the scene so quickly. Had he been headed for his cousin's press conference, as well?

Or had his reasons been more sinister than that?

She suppressed another shiver. "I stopped at the intersection, waiting for a light. There was some kind of commotion in the crowd. Someone dropped something, I think, and while everyone was looking down, someone pushed me into the street. Pushed me hard," she added. "Hard enough to make me fall down. It wasn't an accident."

"You didn't see who it was?"

She shook her head.

"You didn't recognize anyone in the crowd?"

"No."

His dark, probing gaze took her measure. "How long have you been in town, Ms. Snow?"

"How do you know I wasn't born here?" she challenged, flirting with danger.

"You may have been born here, but you haven't lived here in several years. Your accent is, what? Midwestern? Chicago?"

"All right, you caught me," she conceded. "I've only been in Memphis for six weeks."

"What brought you here?"

"I got a job with the *Journal*. I'm a reporter."

His dark eyes met hers. "Made any enemies since you've been here?"

Besides you and your father, you mean? "Reporters

always make enemies," she said. "We wouldn't be doing our job if we didn't."

He gave her a disparaging glance. "What about your private life?"

"Are you asking if I have any jilted lovers lurking about in the bushes?"

He smiled slightly. "Something like that. Jealousy and rejection are powerful motivations. They rank right up there with revenge."

Their gazes collided, and something jolted inside Valerie. Something she wanted to deny, but couldn't.

What is going on here? This man is your enemy, remember?

Or at least, he was the son of her enemy. And if she forgot that fact, all she had to do was look into his eyes.

The devil's eyes...

Must be the painkiller, she decided. The drug had dulled her senses. She'd better get rid of him.

"Look, why don't we cut to the chase here, shall we? You asked if I'd made any enemies since I've been in town. We both know that I have." She ran a tired hand through her tangled hair. "You're Judd Colter's son, aren't you?"

"That's right." His eyes still gave away nothing.

Valerie shrugged. "Then you must know about the article I wrote for the *Journal.* The one about the Kingsley kidnapping. If you really want to find out who pushed me in front of that bus, maybe you should start with the three people I mentioned in that article. Including your own father, Sergeant Colter."

A tiny spark of anger ignited in his eyes, the first emotion he'd shown since he'd walked into her room.

"Are you accusing my father of attempted murder, Ms. Snow?"

When she didn't reply, he said, "It might interest you to know that he recently suffered a stroke. He's a very sick man. He's hardly capable of dressing himself, much less pushing someone in front of a bus."

An image flashed in Valerie's mind of the way Judd Colter had looked that night all those years ago. He'd been a vigorous man, tall and muscular, at the peak of physical conditioning. For a moment she felt… what? Surely not sympathy at the thought of such a man being crippled by a stroke. She remembered her own father and why he had been sent to prison, and she lifted her chin.

"He wouldn't have to do it himself, and in any case, there were others mentioned in the article besides Judd Colter. Your uncle, for instance. Raymond Colter was involved in the Kingsley kidnapping investigation, too, as was Captain Rawlins, an old family friend, I believe. Any one of them could have hired someone to follow me." Her eyes narrowed as she gazed up at him. "As a matter of fact, I can't help wondering what *you* were doing on that street corner, Sergeant Colter."

He cocked his head slightly. "Is that a question or an accusation?"

Valerie shrugged.

"As you said, my cousin is holding a press conference this afternoon. I guess it was just luck that put me at the right place at the right time."

Valerie wasn't sure if there was sarcasm in his voice or not. She gave him a long, hard stare. "Whatever your reason for being there, the fact remains that someone tried to kill me, and I want to know what you're going to do about it."

"I'll file a report as soon as I get back to head-quarters."

She looked at him incredulously. *"That's it?"*

"There'll be an investigation, of course."

"Oh, of course," Valerie retorted cynically. "And I'm sure no stone will be left unturned."

He flipped his notebook closed and put it away. "You don't like cops much, do you?"

"Whatever gave you that idea?"

An ironic smile touched his lips. "Your article, for one thing."

"Then you *did* read it."

"Oh, I read it, all right."

"And what did you think?"

It was his turn to shrug. "I guess it made me wonder what it is you really want."

"That's easy," Valerie told him. "I want justice."

"For whom?"

"Cletus Brown."

He looked at her in disgust. "Cletus Brown kidnapped and murdered a three-year-old boy. Justice was served when my father arrested him. Justice was served when Brown was convicted by a jury of his peers and the judge sentenced him to life in prison without parole."

"The evidence against him was all circumstantial," Valerie said.

"Circumstantial or not, it was pretty convincing as I recall. His own brother-in-law testified against him."

"Yes, because he hated him," Valerie blurted. Then, when she saw Brant looking at her curiously, she tempered her words. "It was no secret. The two of

them didn't get along. Odell Campbell worked for the
Kingsleys as a chauffeur, and he used to throw Cletus
Brown some repair work occasionally, but only because
Cletus was married to his sister. He said so under oath.
He claimed Cletus had been around a few days before
the kidnapping, wanting to borrow money, then asking
all kinds of questions about the big fund-raiser Iris
Kingsley was throwing for her son, wanting to know
about the mansion's security and all that. But it was
always his word against Cletus's. No one else heard the
conversation."

"But why would he lie?" Brant challenged. "Why
would he want to send his own sister's husband to
prison?"

He was still looking at her strangely, and Valerie
realized how close she'd come to blowing her cover. She
would have to be a lot more careful from now on, especially around Brant Colter. She couldn't afford to arouse
his suspicions any more than they already were.

"Two reasons," she forced herself to say evenly. "He
never thought Cletus was good enough for his sister, and
since she wouldn't divorce him, this was a good way to
get rid of him."

A dark brow lifted in skepticism. "And the other
reason?"

"He was paid to lie. He quit his job with the Kingsleys
several months after Cletus Brown was convicted and
sent to prison. He turned up driving a new car, wearing
new clothes, apparently having money to burn. Where
did he get it?"

Brant frowned. "How do you know all this?"

"I'm a reporter. I'm paid to dig up this kind of information. Just like cops are—or should be."

Their gazes clashed again, and beyond the icy surface, Valerie saw smoldering animosity in Brant's dark eyes. Animosity and something else that made her wonder how she could ever have thought him without emotion.

"What about the ransom money that was found in the trunk of Cletus Brown's car?" he demanded. "That's hardly circumstantial."

Valerie folded her arms across her chest. "Why would someone smart enough to kidnap one of the Kingsley twins from his room while an important fund-raiser was going on downstairs be stupid enough to leave fifteen thousand dollars of the ransom money in the trunk of his own car? And what happened to the other four hundred and eighty-five thousand? It never turned up.

"Your father was the only one who knew about that money in Cletus Brown's car. According to his testimony, he received an anonymous tip that led him to Cletus Brown, but the fact was, the two of them already knew each other." Valerie saw surprise flash in Brant's dark eyes before he could hide it, and she smiled in satisfaction. "You didn't know that, did you?"

"Cletus Brown had a prior," Brant said. "My father had arrested him before."

It was Valerie's turn to be surprised. "You knew about that?"

"It was a guess," he admitted. "But I'm right, aren't I? That's why he was a suspect to begin with."

Valerie nodded grudgingly. "He was arrested for petty theft a few months before the kidnapping. He stole ten dollars from the cash register in a gas station to buy his daughter a birthday present. He'd gone in trying to find work. He was desperate."

"Desperation doesn't justify theft, Ms. Snow."

"I didn't say it did," she snapped. "I'm just trying to explain his motivation."

"Why does this case mean so much to you?" Brant asked suddenly. "You're obviously very emotional about it. But a thirty-year-old kidnapping is hardly newsworthy."

Valerie cursed herself for her lack of control. What was it about Brant Colter that made her want to lash out at him? Made her want to scream at him who she really was and then watch his face register the revelation?

Would he be surprised? Undoubtedly. Stunned, would be more like it. They would all be shocked, and not a little horrified, to learn that Cletus Brown's daughter was living among them.

She took a long breath, giving herself a moment to regain her composure. "Anything involving the Kingsleys is always news, and besides, the kidnapping never goes away. Just like the Lindbergh case, people are still fascinated by the story, and everyone has his or her own theory as to what happened back then. Me, I think an innocent man was sent to prison. I think Cletus Brown was framed."

"You're forgetting one little thing, aren't you?" Brant asked impatiently. "Where was the motive? What did my father and the others have to gain by framing Cletus Brown?"

Valerie shrugged. "I explained all that in the article. They'd been humiliated by the press and by the FBI. They'd already botched the ransom drop, and the local media crucified them. The only way to redeem themselves was to make an arrest. And don't forget," she added. "Whoever solved that case would become an instant hero. His career and reputation would be made."

"So where and when did Cletus Brown come into the picture? Did they just pull his name from a hat?" Brant asked facetiously.

"He fit the profile," Valerie said. "He'd been out of work for months. His family was practically destitute, and he and his wife were having problems. And he had a record. But most important of all, he had a tie to the Kingsleys through his brother-in-law, who was more than willing to testify against him."

"Well, I have to say," Brant said with something that might have been grudging admiration, "you appear to have thought this out fairly well. There's only one problem with your theory. You have no proof."

Valerie looked up at him. "Not yet."

"Meaning?"

"That article is just the beginning. I won't give up until I get that proof."

Brant's gaze hardened on her. "And in the meantime, you're perfectly willing to ruin three good men's reputations for the sake of a headline."

"Those three good men once *craved* headlines."

"The Constitution says a man is innocent until proven guilty. Cletus Brown was found guilty in a court of law. You're trying my father in the pages of a sleazy tabloid," Brant accused.

"If your father is innocent, he has nothing to worry about from me," Valerie said. "And neither do you."

"Who says I'm worried?" But the edge in his voice betrayed him. He was as angry as she was—maybe more so. Valerie shivered, wondering if she had awakened the proverbial sleeping giant. She had a feeling she didn't want to be around if and when Brant Colter ever lost his temper completely. He was cold on the outside, but she'd glimpsed a fire inside.

He rose to leave. "I'll get a statement typed up for you to sign as soon as possible. In the meantime, if you think of anything else, give me a call at headquarters."

"Sergeant Colter?"

He paused at the door and glanced back at her.

"If you're not worried, why don't you ask your father about Naomi Gillum?"

His gaze narrowed on her. "What?"

"Ask him about Naomi Gillum. Ask him what happened to her."

THE PRESS CONFERENCE, which had started late, was winding up by the time Brant got to city hall. He stopped at the edge of the crowd, watching his cousin at a podium that had been moved outside, to the top of the building's steps.

"So you're saying there is absolutely no truth to the allegations that appeared in yesterday's *Journal?*" a reporter shouted.

Brant watched as his cousin fielded the question with expert aplomb. "That's exactly what I've been saying since the start of this press conference. I think we're all familiar with the *Journal*'s reputation, gentlemen. And ladies," he added with a smile for the three women reporters in the group. Then his expression turned earnest again. "Just as we're familiar with the reputations of the three men targeted in that article. My father, Raymond Colter, was a policeman for nearly ten years before a bullet in the leg took him off active duty. But did he sit around feeling sorry for himself? He did not. He started a security business, parlaying his expertise in law enforcement into a thriving, successful concern, and he has shared his success with the less fortunate among us, funding community centers and midnight basketball for our inner-city kids.

"Captain Hugh Rawlins, a very close friend of my family's and one of our city's finest and most decorated police officers, has devoted more than forty years of his life to law enforcement.

"And is there anyone among us who hasn't heard of my uncle, Judd Colter, one of the most famous policemen this city, indeed this country, has ever produced? Judd Colter's name is legendary in the ranks of law enforcement everywhere.

"He, along with my father and Hugh Rawlins, has done more to fight crime in this city, more to *prevent* crime, than any three men I can think of, and I have been proud to continue their tradition in the district attorney's office, garnering the highest conviction rate of any prosecutor in the state."

His cousin was a consummate politician, Brant had to admit. Austin had managed to turn what could have been a hostile press conference into a rousing campaign speech.

Contrary to what he'd implied earlier, Brant hadn't even known about the press conference until Valerie Snow had mentioned it. He'd tried not to act surprised because he didn't want her to think the Colters were anything less than unified. But the truth was, he and Austin hadn't been close for a long time. They'd been friends as kids, had gone to Memphis State together, and had graduated from law school the same year. But then a woman had come between them, and they'd never reconciled. They'd gone in completely different directions, both professionally and personally.

Austin had married the woman and gone to work in the D.A.'s office, refining his skills for the political career he'd always dreamed of. And Brant had entered the police academy, much to the chagrin of his father.

Brant grimaced, thinking about the arguments he and his father had had over Brant's decision to become a police officer. Though he hadn't come right out and said it, Brant knew the reason his father hadn't wanted him on the force was because he'd thought Brant didn't have what it took to become a cop.

But Hugh Rawlins had. Hugh was the one who had had faith in Brant. Hugh was the one who had taken him under his wing in the department, shown him the ropes and made sure Brant was eventually welcomed into the Brotherhood. The fact was, Hugh Rawlins had been more of a father to Brant than Judd Colter ever was.

But in spite of everything, Brant knew his father had been a good cop—the best—and he couldn't believe the things Valerie Snow had written about him. Or about any of them.

The problem was she seemed convinced of her own story.

And someone *had* pushed her in front of a bus this afternoon.

The press conference ended, and Austin's wife, Kristin, joined him at the podium. They made a striking couple—Austin with the Colter dark hair and dark eyes, and Kristin, a beautiful, blue-eyed blonde. No one would have guessed that two months ago, the two had been separated, and that Kristin had called Brant night and day, trying to worm her way back into his good graces.

And into his bed.

As Brant turned away, he saw Hugh Rawlins standing at the fringes of the crowd. He was in uniform, his hat pulled low over his eyes, so that he wouldn't be recognized. Brant walked over to him.

"Some show, huh?" Hugh clapped a hand on Brant's shoulder. "Austin's going to make a helluva congressman."

"A helluva politician, anyway," Brant conceded. "What are you doing here?"

Hugh shrugged. He wasn't a tall man, nor was he particularly muscular. Rather he was of average height and average weight, his appearance completely nondescript except for one distinguishing feature—a jagged scar ran the length of the right side of his face, from his temple to his chin, turning what otherwise would have been a pleasant face into one that looked faintly menacing.

His hand tightened on Brant's shoulder. "Let's walk," he said.

They headed toward Main Street, which in the seventies had become the Mid-America Mall in an attempt to revitalize downtown. Hugh stopped at a stone bench and propped one foot on the seat. He leaned his arms across his leg, gazing at the pigeons who were busily pecking at a bag of popcorn someone had thrown at a trash bin.

"I was still at headquarters when you called in earlier," Hugh said. "I heard about the Snow woman. How bad was it?"

"Not as bad as it could have been," Brant told him. "A few cuts and bruises. Nothing too serious."

"What happened?"

"She says she was pushed in front of a bus."

Hugh turned to Brant. "Think she's lying?"

Brant bent to pick up a stray popcorn kernel and tossed it at the pigeons. "As a matter of fact, I'm inclined to believe her. She definitely fell in front of that bus, and she doesn't strike me as the clumsy or careless type."

"Did she give you any idea who might want to harm her?"

Brant thought about what she'd said. *If you really want to find out who pushed me in front of that bus, why don't you start with the three people I mentioned in that article? Including your own father, Sergeant Colter.*

"Not really," he said.

"Did you see anything?" It might have been Brant's imagination, but he thought Hugh looked a little anxious.

The strain was probably getting to him, Brant decided. Scandal in the police force was nothing new, but as far as Brant could remember, no dirt had ever touched Hugh's name. He was a cop's cop, having started on the street and risen through the ranks the hard way. While Judd Colter had commanded respect and admiration, even awe at times, from his fellow officers, Hugh Rawlins was a man they could like. A man just like themselves.

"I'm not sure," Brant said. "Do you remember a snitch named Remy Devereaux? Dad used him on occasion."

Hugh looked surprised. "Remy Devereaux? He left town years ago. Why do you ask?"

"I thought I saw him on that street corner," Brant said grimly.

Hugh turned back to the pigeons. "I doubt that. Word had it that the reason he left town was because he got into some trouble with the Mob. I don't think he'd come back to Memphis."

"You're probably right. But it sure did look like him," Brant said.

Hugh, still not looking up, asked, "What were *you* doing on that street corner, Brant?"

For a moment, Brant thought about telling him what Valerie Snow had assumed—that he'd been going to Austin's press conference. But then he shrugged and said, "I was following her."

"Why?"

"I guess I wanted to see if she was the monster everyone seems to think she is."

Hugh straightened from the bench and turned to face him. "How did you know who she was?"

"I called the *Journal*'s offices from my cell phone. They said she was just leaving the building. Two women came out, and—don't ask me how—I knew immediately which one was her." The truth was, he'd known the moment he'd laid eyes on Valerie Snow that she meant trouble.

"Did she have horns sprouting from her head or something?" Hugh joked.

Brant grinned. "Hardly. I guess I figured eventually to catch up with her and ask her a few questions, but then all hell broke loose."

"Yeah," was Hugh's only comment.

"Anyway," Brant continued, "I'd like to stay on this case."

Hugh frowned. "That might constitute conflict of interest."

"She didn't seem overly concerned about that," Brant said. "I'd really like to follow up on this."

"I'll talk to Lieutenant Bermann," Hugh offered, referring to Brant's immediate superior in Robbery and Homicide. "We'll see what he says."

"Thanks."

"You know, I'm glad the woman wasn't seriously hurt," Hugh said slowly. "But maybe this'll put an end to her accusations. Maybe she'll be frightened enough to want to drop the whole thing."

"I don't think so," Brant replied, troubled by Hugh's comments. "She's determined to find proof that will clear Cletus Brown."

Hugh glanced at him in alarm. "Proof? What the hell kind of proof could she find?"

"Have you ever heard of a woman named Naomi Gillum?"

Something flashed in Hugh's eyes before he quickly looked away. His gaze scoured the street in front of them. "No, can't say as I have. Why?"

"Valerie Snow mentioned her."

Hugh shrugged. "Name doesn't ring a bell."

His response sounded convincing enough, but just before he'd voiced the denial, Brant could have sworn that what he'd seen in Hugh Rawlins's eyes was fear.

CHAPTER THREE

"WHAT ARE YOU SAYING, exactly? That someone tried to kill you? *Murder* you, for God's sake?" Julian Temple's eyes gleamed gleefully at the prospect.

"That's what I'm saying." Valerie tried not to be offended by her boss's reaction as she sat across from his desk the next day. She supposed she could hardly expect less from the "King of Sleaze." At the age of forty, the owner and editor-in-chief of the *Journal* thrived on sensationalism and scandal, the uglier the better.

It was for that reason that Valerie, with her graduate degree in journalism from Northwestern and her years of serious reporting with the *Sun-Times,* had been squeamish about joining a tabloid-style paper like the *Journal.*

But it was also for that reason that she'd sought out Julian when she'd first arrived in Memphis. She'd known that no reputable paper would touch the story she wanted to write, not with the limited amount of evidence—mostly from undocumented sources—that she'd been able to gather so far.

The story she wanted to tell about the Kingsley kidnapping was just the sort of thing Julian Temple loved. In fact, he'd practically been salivating after that first meeting, when she'd outlined for him what she wanted to do. He'd loved the prospect of implicating a few of the old-guard police force—not to mention a local entrepreneur and philanthropist.

And the Kingsleys, with their money and power and political clout, were a tabloid's gold mine, from the tragic kidnapping thirty-one years ago, to Edward Kingsley's rise and fall in politics, to the exploits of his son, Andrew, the surviving Kingsley twin.

The Kingsleys were the stuff headlines and scandal were made of, and Julian had given Valerie carte blanche from the moment he'd hired her.

It was ironic, Valerie thought, because with his blond hair and movie-star good looks, Julian hardly looked the part of gossipmonger. And he certainly didn't have that kind of background. He was from a very wealthy, old-money Nashville family who had bought him the *Journal* as a graduation present when he'd left Harvard, expecting him to turn it into a daily that would compete with the *Press Scimitar* and the *Commercial Appeal*.

Julian, however, had had other ideas, and while his family might not agree with his methods, they could hardly argue with his success.

He grinned at Valerie, not bothering to conceal his relish for what she had just told him. "Well, well, well. I'd say your little article has hit a nerve, Val."

"To say the least," she agreed. "And I'm fine, thank you. The bus didn't touch me."

"Oh, sorry." Julian waved an impatient hand. "But that's obvious, isn't it? You wouldn't be here otherwise."

"I did go to the emergency room," she reminded him. "Where I was interrogated by Judd Colter's son, I might add."

Julian's eyes widened. "You're kidding. What was he doing there?"

"That's what I'd like to know. He says he was going to his cousin's press conference, but I'm not so sure. I mean, he was right *there*. His was the first face I saw when I came to." Valerie shivered in spite of herself, thinking about those black eyes staring down at her.

She'd even dreamed about him last night, a disturbing turn of events. The nightmares she'd had about his father were one thing, but the dream she'd had about Brant Colter was something else entirely.

The erotic images swept through her mind now, causing her face to heat unexpectedly. She fervently hoped Julian wouldn't notice, but she needn't have worried. His mind was off on a different tangent altogether.

"You think *he* could have been the one to push you in front of that bus? You know…acting on his father's behalf, or something? I hear Judd Colter's been ill recently."

"He had a stroke," Valerie said.

"Whatever. In any case, you've got the makings of a real headliner here. Distraught Son Tries to Protect Dying Father's Reputation. Cop's Outrage Turns Deadly. Something like that. You get my drift."

Loud and clear, Valerie thought. She rubbed her throbbing temples with her fingertips. Julian always gave her a headache.

He snapped his fingers suddenly and rummaged through the pile of papers on his desk. "I almost forgot," he said, handing her a pink message slip. "Blackman called."

Harry Blackman was a local P.I. Julian had suggested she use. Valerie had been skeptical at first, wondering if anyone Julian recommended could be trusted, but so far, Harry Blackman had proved to be reliable as well as resourceful.

"What did he say?" Valerie asked, glancing down at the paper.

"He's got something for you. He wants to meet with you tonight in his office."

Valerie's initial excitement vanished. "Tonight? Why not sooner? I'm not exactly crazy about going into his neighborhood after dark."

"Has to be tonight. He's out of the office all day, on some Motel Eight surveillance job or something. His associate doesn't spell him until seven."

"All right," Valerie said. "If that's the way it has to be."

"Look, I'd go with you," Julian said, "but I've already made plans for tonight. Tomorrow night, however, I'm free as a bird, and I'd like for you to accompany me to Austin Colter's fund-raiser at the Kingsley mansion." He dangled two tickets in front of her, and Valerie reached across the desk to snatch them out of his hand.

"How did you get these? The *Journal* is definitely persona non grata in his campaign camp right now."

Julian shrugged. "My family still has some pretty important contacts in the state. I had my old man call in a few favors. Besides, at five thousand bucks a ticket, they can't afford to be choosy. I'll pick you up at eight. It's black tie, by the way."

"Should be a night to remember," she said, wondering if Brant would be there. Somehow a black-tie fund-raiser hardly seemed his scene, but then, what did she really know about Judd Colter's son?

AT SEVEN O'CLOCK that evening, Valerie left the *Journal*'s offices, climbed into her dark blue Ford Explorer and headed toward the river.

Brant pulled into traffic behind her, keeping enough distance between her Explorer and his city vehicle—a beige, nondescript sedan—so he wouldn't be detected. He had no idea what her destination might be, but he knew that, one way or another, she was headed for trouble.

It was ironic. She'd written an article trying to destroy his father's reputation, and now he'd been put in the precarious position of trying to protect her.

Fate, he reflected, could sure as hell play some bad jokes.

She was a good driver, he noted as she wove in and out of traffic like a pro. On first glance, he would have pegged her as the sports-car type, in something sleek and red, something fast and dangerous; but then, when he'd seen her climb into the Explorer, he'd decided that maybe she had a practical side after all.

He hoped to hell he could appeal to that practical side now, make her see reason. If someone *was* trying to kill her, she didn't appear to be taking any precautions.

Instead, she turned toward the river, heading for a section of downtown that no one, least of all a woman, should be going to alone. It would be dark soon. She should be home, safe and sound, watching television or reading a good book. Not traipsing about in a dangerous part of town.

But then, he had to admit, a part of him was glad that she was. A part of him was as intrigued as hell by Valerie Snow's daring.

She pulled into a parking lot, paid the attendant, then

headed across the street to a dingy office building that had once been a cotton warehouse. Some of the warehouses along the river had been turned into posh professional buildings and studio apartments, but no one had bothered to renovate the ones in this area. They didn't have views of the river, but were bordered by alleys that led to more warehouses at the back.

She entered the building, and Brant quickly parked and followed her inside. The elevator door was closing as he walked into the dim, unattended lobby. A bank of mailboxes lined a wall across from a wooden stairway that led to the upper floors. Brant checked the boxes, looking for a name he might recognize. Blackman Security, on the fifth floor, caught his attention.

Harry Blackman was a security expert who used to work for his uncle Raymond. According to Raymond, Harry Blackman had once been the best in the business, but a drinking problem had led to his downfall, and Raymond had had to fire him. Their relationship had ended with bad feelings all around, and since then, Harry had become a small-time P.I., sometimes con man, hustling work wherever he could get it. He'd had run-ins with the police department more than once.

Brant checked the other businesses in the building, but none of them—independent insurance agents and accountants, for the most part—seemed likely prospects. If Valerie was mixed up with the likes of Harry Blackman, she didn't know what she was getting herself into.

Brant started up the stairs, but a shadow moved by one of the grimy windows, drawing his attention. Probably a vagrant, he decided, or someone who worked in one of the warehouses at the back, but still, it wouldn't hurt to check it out. Valerie was upstairs and would likely be there for several more minutes.

Brant hurried outside and entered the alley. Though darkness fell late in July, the street was full of shadows. Most of the evening traffic had long since disappeared from this part of town. Only the homeless and druggies looking for a fix would be caught out after dark down here.

And cops following beautiful women, Brant thought, hugging the warehouse as he made his way to the back of the building.

He stood still for a moment, listening to the darkness. A faint clanging sound came to him, drawing his attention upward. A metal fire escape led to the upper floors, and he thought he detected a movement on one of the landings.

Without a second thought, Brant started climbing.

HARRY BLACKMAN was probably the most formidable-looking man Valerie had ever met. It wasn't just the fact that he was huge—well over six feet and at least two hundred and fifty pounds of solid muscle—nor the fact that his head was completely bald with a dagger tattooed at the back.

What Valerie found so intimidating was the fact that he always wore a weapon, a .357 Colt Python strapped to his side, in plain view. She had no idea if he carried the weapon on the street or not, or whether he even had a permit for it. She'd never met him any place other than his office, and the gun was always there, like a crucial appendage he couldn't live without.

Valerie supposed it was the nature of his occupation, or perhaps the location of his office, that made Harry overly cautious, but whatever the case, she found it hard to keep her mind—and her eyes—off that gun.

"All right, here's the deal," he said, in a voice that sounded like two sheets of sandpaper being rubbed together. "I've located the woman you're after. She's in New Orleans."

Valerie's heart quickened. "*Is?* That means she's still alive?"

He nodded. "She's going by the name Marie LaPierre. Has been for over twenty-five years. She owns a voodoo shop in the Quarter."

A voodoo shop? Somehow that seemed appropriate to Valerie. There were so many strange things about her father's case.

"Here's the address." Harry shoved a crumpled piece of paper across the desk toward her. Valerie noticed, as she had before, the tiny tattoos on each of his knuckles, but she'd never been able to tell what the images were.

"The guy you're looking for. This Odell Campbell. He's in a nursing home in Madison, a small town fifty miles north of here. He's suffering from Alzheimer's, the advanced stages, so I doubt he'll be able to tell you much."

Valerie's heart sank at that news. She'd hoped to be able to convince her uncle to tell the truth after all these years. He was her mother's brother, so he had to have some goodness in him. But now it looked as if it didn't matter whether he did or not. Odell would, in all likelihood, be of no use to her.

Still, Valerie took the address of the nursing home from Harry. She knew she would pay her uncle a visit for one simple reason: other than her father, he was the only living relative she had left on this earth.

"What was that?" Harry said.

"What was what?" So lost in thought had Valerie been, she had no idea what he was talking about.

Harry stood and drew his weapon. Valerie gasped, but he motioned for silence just as the window behind him shattered.

"Get down!" he shouted, plastering himself against the wall.

He didn't have to tell her twice. Valerie hit the floor behind Harry's desk as he reached over and turned off the light. The office fell into darkness, but enough illumination filtered in through the broken window that Valerie could see Harry silhouetted against the wall. He was moving toward the window, but another shot rang out, and he fell back for just a split second, then sprang forward, firing through the broken glass.

Valerie huddled against the desk, her hands over her ears, her heart pounding in terror. She looked up to see Harry heading toward the door.

"Harry!"

"Stay there," he ordered. "He's going in through a window. I'm going after him."

"But—"

Harry disappeared through the door, and Valerie was left alone in the darkness. She wondered what she should do. Harry had told her to stay put, but she didn't like the idea of remaining here in the dark, all by herself, while someone who had been shooting at either Harry or her or both of them roamed the building.

She would make a run for it, Valerie decided. Get to her car.

No, maybe she should use the phone. Call the police. But then, she didn't exactly trust the police, did she?

All right, then, she would run for it. Done.

She edged to the end of the desk and peered around, toward the window. Someone was easing over the ledge, and for a moment, relief surged through her. "Harry," she whispered. Then the man straightened, and she realized he was as tall as Harry, but not nearly as bulky.

The man stood for a moment, looking around, getting his bearings. Then, very deliberately, he moved toward the door. Valerie flattened herself against the desk, praying he wouldn't see her.

As he passed by her, something triggered a flash of recognition inside Valerie. Suddenly she knew the man inside the office with her was Brant Colter. For a moment, she started to call out, but then she realized that his movements were suspect, to say the least. What was he doing here, in Harry Blackman's office, moments after she'd been shot at?

He opened the door into the hallway, looked out, and then, in a heartbeat, was gone. Valerie sat huddled on the floor, her heart beating a rapid staccato inside her.

Brant Colter was *here*. Just like he'd been on the scene the day she'd been pushed in front of the bus. Had he been the one shooting into the office just minutes ago?

She got to her feet and stood in the darkness. She had to get out of here. Now. Her every instinct screamed in warning, and Valerie wasn't one to ignore them. Crossing the floor to the door, she peered into the corridor. It was empty. The doors that opened to the other offices were all closed, and only a dim light near the elevator illuminated the gloomy hallway.

She started down the corridor when she heard the unmistakable clang of the elevator, and saw the Up arrow lit. Someone was heading up to the fifth floor. But who? Harry? Brant Colter coming back? Or was there a third person in the building? The gunman?

Valerie whirled and ran down the hallway toward Harry's office. She vaguely recalled seeing the stairwell door somewhere off to her left, and she tried all the doors along the way until she found one that was unlocked. She pushed it open just as the elevator came to a halt and the doors slid open.

Trying not to make a sound, Valerie stood just inside the stairwell, leaving the door opened a crack so that she could look out. Someone hurried down the corridor. As he drew even with Harry's door, he paused for a moment, and Valerie held her breath, wondering if he had heard the pounding of her heart in the darkness of the stairwell.

She didn't recognize the man. He kept his face averted, so that she couldn't see his features, but Valerie had the distinct impression from the way he stood that he was a good deal older than either Brant or Harry.

He carried a gun, and as Valerie stood watching him, she saw him check the clip with a smooth, practiced motion that made her wonder how often he'd done that very same thing in the past. Could he be a professional hit man? Hired to get rid of her?

The thought was almost her undoing. Her hand, sweaty with fear, slipped on the doorknob, and the door clicked shut. Even as slight as it was, there was no mistaking the sound, and Valerie knew she'd given herself away. She turned and headed for the stairs, slipping off her shoes as she ran.

Instead of going down, she went up. The gunman

would expect her to try and reach the street, wouldn't he? By going up, she hoped she could lose him.

In stocking feet, she flew up the stairs and pulled open the door to the roof. It was hot and muggy outside. The low-hanging clouds over the river were heavy with moisture. Thunder rumbled in the distance, and Valerie knew there would be rain soon. She wondered if that would help or hinder her escape. She wondered where Harry was. And Brant Colter. Was he working with the gunman? Were the two of them stalking her together?

Valerie didn't dare stop to think about her predicament. She had to concentrate on finding a way out of here.

She hurried to the side of the building and looked over. The wall was smooth and sheer, five stories to the ground. There had to be a fire escape around here somewhere, she thought. Another warehouse backed up against this one, and an eight-foot gulf separated the two roofs. For a moment, Valerie contemplated jumping across, but even though she'd never been afraid of heights, the gap looked wider by the moment.

She turned and started toward the other side just as the roof door opened. The opening lay in shadow, but she saw the gunman standing in the doorway. She couldn't see his face, but she saw him lift his hand as he spotted her.

Valerie heard a soft, spitting sound as a silenced bullet whizzed by her ear like a bee. She turned and charged back to the edge of the roof. There was no other way, no time to warn herself she might not be able to make it. She caught her breath, and before she had time to think, she was flying through space as the wall of the second building rushed to meet her.

If she hadn't panicked at the last second, she would have cleared the space with room to spare. As it was, she began to reach for a handhold before she'd made it across. Her momentum slowed, and Valerie grabbed desperately for the edge of the roof.

And missed.

CHAPTER FOUR

THE IMPACT JARRED her body as she slammed into the wall. She screamed and closed her eyes as her arms flailed wildly for purchase.

Then, miraculously, someone grabbed her. A hand closed around one of her wrists like a vise, and Valerie dangled in midair. Her head spun dizzily as she heard a familiar voice say, "Don't look down. I've got you."

Valerie looked up. She couldn't see his face in the darkness, but she knew who he was. Brant Colter had saved her life.

Or had he? How much longer would he hold on to her?

With her other arm, Valerie reached out and grabbed a drainpipe.

"Let go," Brant said. "I'll pull you up."

Let go? Not in this lifetime. Valerie closed her eyes, willing her strength. Her arms were on fire. She knew she wouldn't be able to hang on much longer. In fact, if it weren't for Brant's grip on her wrist, she might already have plunged to her death.

But still, something wouldn't let her release the drainpipe. Something wouldn't let her trust Brant Colter.

"We can't stay out here like this all night," he said impatiently. "In case you hadn't noticed, someone was shooting at you a minute ago."

"Was it you?" Valerie gasped.

"Yeah, that makes sense." His breath was beginning to tell from the strain. "I shoot at you one minute, and the next, I'm trying to keep you from falling off a roof. Now, turn loose before we both hit the pavement."

In spite of herself, Valerie glanced down. She couldn't help herself. The ground seemed a million miles away. "How do I know you won't drop me?" she asked desperately.

"I guess you'll just have to trust me, won't you?"

Valerie's fingers slipped on the drainpipe. She was hanging on by hardly more than her imagination. "I'm falling," she whispered. "Oh, God—"

Just as her fingers slid from the pipe, Brant grabbed her other wrist, gave a mighty heave, and pulled her to safety. Valerie scrambled over the edge of the building and collapsed, panting from exertion and terror.

"Come on," Brant said, tugging her to her feet. "It's not a good idea for us to stay out here in the open."

"I don't hear any gunshots," Valerie said weakly, allowing herself to be pulled up and along the roof toward the opposite side. "Maybe he gave up and left."

"Maybe," Brant said, but he didn't sound too confident. "There should be a fire escape around here somewhere. Let's find it before he does."

"Who's 'he'?"

There was a slight hesitation before Brant said, "I was hoping you could tell me."

"You're the cop. I'm just a reporter." A very frightened reporter.

"You don't have any idea who might want you dead?"

"I've already told you what I think," Valerie said.

Brant located the fire escape and started over the side of the building, but her words stopped him. A break in the clouds allowed enough moonlight to filter through so that she could see his face. His eyes.

She shivered.

"I can assure you it wasn't my father chasing you over that roof. He can hardly walk across a room without a cane these days."

"Yes, but as I pointed out yesterday," Valerie replied, trying to ignore the coldness in his dark gaze, "he wouldn't have to do it himself, would he? Your father must have a lot of contacts, on both sides of the law."

She could sense his anger in the darkness. It was almost a tangible thing, and yet there was another emotion that was perhaps even stronger. Valerie would almost have named it doubt—or even fear—if she didn't know better. "We obviously aren't going to come to any agreement on this subject tonight, so why don't we concentrate on getting out of here in one piece? Agreed?"

Valerie took a deep breath. "Agreed."

He extended his hand. "Come on, then."

Reluctantly, she reached out and took his hand. At the very moment her fingers touched his, a clap of thunder rolled across the heavens as the storm neared downtown. Valerie jumped back, as if she'd been burned.

"It was just thunder," Brant said, obviously mistaking her reaction for fear.

"I—I'm glad it wasn't a gunshot," Valerie muttered. She ignored Brant's offer of help and grabbed the ladder, stepping cautiously onto the first rung. The metal stair was fastened directly into the brick wall and looked as old as the building itself. Valerie fervently hoped the fasteners would hold. It had probably been years since the ladder had taken any weight.

The metal creaked and moaned as they descended. Valerie was very aware of Brant, going down the steps in front of her. If he looked up, he would have an unobstructed view of her legs. For some reason, the thought made shivers run up and down her spine.

When they neared the ground, Brant jumped from the ladder, then placed his hands around her waist and lifted her down, holding her for a fraction longer than was necessary. Valerie turned in his arms and looked up at him.

A flash of lightning illuminated his face briefly, so that Valerie could see the distinct angles and planes of his features, the tiny cleft in his chin, the darkness of his eyes. She'd seen that face in her nightmares for more than thirty years, but it had never frightened her more than it did at this moment.

She had the wildest notion that he was going to try and kiss her, and wondered what she would do if he did. Push him away? She wanted to believe that she would, but at the moment, that didn't seem a likely prospect. Not with her heart pounding away inside her. Not with her skin tingling in awareness where he touched her.

"We shouldn't be here like this," he said softly. "It's too dangerous."

"I know." Her teeth chattered in spite of the heat. He wasn't talking about the gunman, and they both knew it. But he took her arm anyway, and pulled her into the deeper shadows of the building. As quietly as they could, they made their way around to the street.

"Where do you think Harry is?" Valerie whispered.

Brant shrugged. "Harry Blackman can take care of himself. Right now, we have to get you out of here."

"How do you know Harry?" she asked in surprise.

"I could ask you the same thing," he said dryly. "But another time. Come on."

He pulled her out of the shadows, and they ran across the street to the parking lot. Valerie dug her keys out of her purse and used the remote to unlock her car. Brant opened the door for her, and she slid in.

"Aren't you coming?" she asked in alarm.

"Not yet." When she hesitated he said, "Get out of here. Hurry."

"But—"

"Go." He slammed the door and stepped back. Valerie started the engine and peeled out of the parking lot. In her rearview mirror, she saw Brant run across the street, heading back to the warehouse.

Was he searching for the gunman? she wondered. Or meeting an accomplice?

BRANT DREW HIS GUN and entered the building through the front door. He paused at the foot of the stairs, listening for sounds of the intruder, but all he heard was the dull hum of the air-conditioning system. He started up, watching the shadowy corners and crevices above him. When he got to the fifth floor, he pushed open the stairwell door and peered out into the deserted hallway.

As he stood listening, faint sounds came to him from the end of the corridor. Shuffling papers. A voice muttering an oath. Brant stepped cautiously out of the stairwell and made his way down the hall to the open door of Harry Blackman's office.

Blackman stood behind his desk, cursing a blue

streak as he flung files around the office helter-skelter. A small trickle of blood oozed down the side of his face unnoticed.

For a moment, Brant went unnoticed, too. Then Blackman looked up and saw his gun.

"Well, hell," he said and sat down heavily in his chair. "Who are you?"

"Police officer," Brant replied, flashing his badge.

"Who the hell called the cops?" Blackman demanded. "The chick? Where is she?"

"Safe, for the moment. And no one called me," Brant said. "I was in the area and heard shots."

Blackman gave him a skeptical look. "No cop is ever in this area unless he has extracurricular business to attend to." His gaze narrowed. "Wait a minute. Wait just a damned minute. I know you."

"Sergeant Brant Colter. Memphis Police Department."

"*Colter. I knew it.*" A string of expletives burst from Blackman's mouth. He looked at Brant in disgust. "You wouldn't happen to be Raymond Colter's boy, would you?"

"Nephew." Brant put away his gun and walked into the office, stopping just short of Blackman's desk, which was littered with papers and files.

Blackman sat back in his chair and steepled his fingers beneath his chin. "That's right," he mused. "Raymond's boy is some kind of hotshot D.A. or something. I read about him in the paper the other day. Said he's running for Congress. Who would have thought a little snot-nosed brat like him would have ever amounted to a hill of beans? But then, that kid had the makings of a politician, even back when I worked for Raymond.

Always real devious-like. Always snooping around in other people's business."

If Blackman expected Brant to come to his cousin's defense, he was in for a big surprise. "Looks like you took a pretty mean hit," he said grimly. "Mind telling me what happened here?"

"You know as much as I do," Blackman growled. "You heard the shots. Someone fired into my window. I went after him, he coldcocked me and got away. End of story. At least until I get my hands on the slimy little bas—"

"Did you get a look at him?"

Blackman shook his head. "Hell, no. Sucker jumped me from behind. Hit me in the back of the head."

"Then how did you cut your forehead."

Blackman's expression grew even darker. "I was standing at the top of the stairs when he jumped me. Damned lucky I didn't break my neck." He wiped a sleeve across the cut without flinching.

Blackman was tough, no question. At least two hundred and fifty pounds of solid muscle. Taking him out, even from behind and in darkness, would have been no mean feat. It would have been easier just to shoot him, but obviously, he hadn't been the target.

Which meant Valerie had been.

"What kind of work are you doing for Valerie Snow?" Brant asked.

"That's privileged information."

"This is a police investigation. Valerie Snow's life is in danger, and I'd appreciate your cooperation. In fact, I'm going to have to demand it."

"That so?" Blackman leaned forward, his eyes flashing fire. "All right, let me level with you, then. Valerie

Snow has a thing about the police. She doesn't trust cops, especially ones named Colter, and neither do I. Your uncle did a real number on me, and I haven't forgotten. You're the last person I'd tell squat to."

Brant could feel his own temper rising, but he tried to hold it in check. "You may not have a choice. I could get a warrant to search your office, seize your files, shut you down indefinitely. In short, I could make your life miserable, Blackman, if I've a mind to."

Blackman cocked a dark brow. "Yeah? Well, what else is new. The cops have been harassing me for years, ever since Raymond fired me. If you've got questions, you go to my client for answers. But I doubt she'll tell *you* anything."

Brant doubted it, too. Blackman was right. Valerie Snow didn't trust him, and for one simple reason: he was Judd Colter's son.

He had a sudden flash of the way she'd looked earlier, gazing up at him. The way she'd felt in his arms. He'd wanted to kiss her. He couldn't remember the last time he'd wanted to kiss a woman so badly. She was beautiful and mysterious and tough as nails. A potentially lethal combination if Brant had ever seen one, but that knowledge didn't lessen his attraction for her. Just the opposite, in fact.

Who was she? he wondered again. Who was she, really?

Brant started to question Blackman further, but then he spotted the corner of a file jutting out from beneath Blackman's desk. Brant stooped and picked it up, glancing at the handwritten label on the folder. *Naomi Gillum.*

He handed the folder to Blackman. "This what you're looking for?"

Blackman grabbed the file and opened it. The contents, whatever they had been, were missing, and with another explosion of expletives, Blackman flung the empty folder to the floor.

VALERIE LET HERSELF into her duplex and turned off the alarm system, thankful she'd had the presence of mind to have one installed when she'd first moved in. Her apartment had been broken into numerous times in Chicago, and she'd learned the hard way that a good security system could save a lot of wear and tear on her nerves.

Well, her nerves had certainly taken a beating tonight, she thought wearily, slipping out of her shoes as she headed for the kitchen. Someone had shot into Harry Blackman's office while she'd been inside. There was a chance, of course, that Harry had been the target, but she didn't think that was likely. Not after the bus incident yesterday.

Twice. Twice in two days her life had been threatened.

Or maybe someone was just trying to scare her. When she thought about it, that seemed the more reasonable possibility. After all, she lived alone. Other than the alarm system, she took no particular safety precautions. If someone really wanted to kill her, would it be all that difficult to do?

Valerie shivered. In fact, it would be quite easy. She *was* all alone. She could go missing for days, and there wouldn't be a single, solitary soul to look for her. To ask questions. To worry and wonder about her whereabouts.

The only person who had ever really cared about her was her mother, and she was gone now. Valerie had no one.

No, that wasn't really true, she thought, as she poured herself a glass of wine. Her father cared about her. At least, he once had. Maybe he would again if she were to free him from prison.

Is that the real reason why you're doing this? she asked herself grimly, pausing to stare at her reflection in the window above the sink. *So you won't be alone?*

Valerie wanted to believe her motives were completely altruistic: that she was working to free her father because he was an innocent man. Truth to be told, however, she knew her reasoning was a lot more complicated than that. She knew that freeing her father was a way of freeing herself—from the feelings of guilt and unworthiness that had followed her throughout her entire life.

Wasn't that why she had yet to go see her father, to confide to him what she was doing? To ask for his help? It wasn't really to spare his feelings or to keep from giving him false hope, as she'd told herself. It was because she was afraid to face him. Afraid to look into his eyes. Afraid of what she might see.

"He is innocent," she whispered, and repeated the mantra in her head as she'd done many times in the last six weeks. Then, as if to further affirm her conviction, she opened one of the canisters on the kitchen counter and removed her mother's diary, leafing through the pages, tracing with her fingertip the words she now knew by heart.

Cletus was not always the best husband to me nor the perfect father to our little Violet, though I know he loved her as much as I do. Maybe more so, because he was willing to go to prison in order to save her life.

A man like that can't be a murderer. I know, with every fiber of my being, that he did not kidnap that poor little boy. He did not murder Adam Kingsley.

The police set him up to take the fall, and my own brother, God have mercy on his soul, helped them do it.

I can do nothing but sit by helplessly, day after day, month after month, year after year, while Cletus's life slowly slips away in that awful place.

If I came forward, even now, and told the police what I know, not only would Cletus's life be in danger, but so would mine and Violet's.

That's why we left Memphis in the first place, why I had to sever all ties with Cletus. Because the threat is still there. The men who framed Cletus would do anything, even murder an innocent child, to keep the truth from coming out.

Only in the pages of my journal, where I know no eyes but my own will see these words, can I reveal the secret of what happened the night Adam Kingsley was kidnapped.

A newspaper clipping slipped from the pages of the diary and floated to the floor. Valerie knelt and picked it up, spreading the article open on the tiny bar that separated the kitchen from the living area. She stared down at the yellowed newspaper photo of herself and Sergeant Judd Colter.

In all these years, Valerie had never forgotten the way Judd Colter had looked at her the night her father had been arrested, the terror he had instilled in her. Only when the cameras had been trained on him outside their home had he shown her kindness and compassion. Only then had he acted as though Valerie were anything more consequential to him than a speck of dust.

He'd used those cameras to his advantage. He'd used *her,* and for that Valerie despised him. For that, he would have to pay.

She took a sip of her wine, grimacing at the bitter taste. Judd Colter had fooled a lot of people back then, but he'd never fooled her. The image he portrayed to the public was very different from the man who had terrorized her family. She'd seen the other side of him that night. The dark side.

Valerie shivered, remembering the coldness in his eyes.

Remembering her hatred of him.

Remembering what she had to do.

Unbidden, an image of Brant Colter materialized in her mind. She thought about the way her heart had quickened at his nearness earlier, the way her stomach had fluttered in awareness when he'd looked at her. The way she'd wanted him to kiss her.

But how could she possibly be attracted to a man who looked so very much like Judd Colter? How could she even entertain the notion that he might not be like his father? He was a Colter, wasn't he? He was a cop. They were all the same. They stuck up for each other.

They protected one another at any cost, even if it meant sending an innocent man to prison.

Even if it meant threatening a woman and her small child.

Was Brant Colter really any different? When push came to shove, regardless of what she found out, would he side with her against his family, his friends, his own father?

Valerie very much doubted it.

The doorbell rang, and she jumped, startled from her reverie by the unexpected sound. Cautiously, she walked to the front window and glanced out. A beige sedan she didn't recognize was parked in her driveway.

She glanced at her watch. It was after ten. Who would be visiting her at this time of night? She had no friends in town except for Angie, who was out of town tonight, and Julian Temple, who drove a Mercedes.

Valerie stepped back from the window, unsure what to do. Call the police?

And tell them what? That someone was ringing her doorbell?

A would-be murderer wasn't likely to do that, was he?

The doorbell sounded once more, and Valerie jumped again. Hand at her throat, she peered through the peephole. Brant's distorted image stared back at her.

"Valerie? Open up! We need to talk." His deep voice vibrated through the wooden door, sending shivers of alarm through Valerie. She could imagine what that voice would do to her in the dead of night, with no one around but the two of them…

"Valerie, come on! I know you're in there. Don't you want to hear what happened tonight?"

Taking a deep breath, Valerie opened the door and drew it back. He stood on the other side, his expression grave as he stared down at her. For a moment, neither of them spoke. Valerie's heart began to pound inside her at the grimness of his features. The darkness of his gaze.

Then he pushed past her and walked inside.

Valerie closed the door and followed him. "What happened?" she asked anxiously. "Did you get the shooter? Did you see Harry?"

"Harry's fine," Brant answered wearily. "But the gunman got away."

"That was convenient," Valerie said dryly.

"What's that supposed to mean?"

She shrugged. "It might be better for you that he got away."

His gaze hardened on her. "I assume you're implying that you think my father—or my uncle or my friend or all of them—had something to do with the shooting."

Valerie shrugged. "They were all three involved in the Kingsley kidnapping investigation. They arrested Cletus Brown. They were responsible for sending him to prison. They're the only ones I can think of who wouldn't want the truth to come out."

"And you think they'd be willing to kill you to silence you." There was something in his eyes that made Valerie's uneasiness grow. Why had she let this man into her home? He was a Colter, for God's sake. How could she trust him?

"I think they're trying to silence me, all right," Valerie said and walked over to the bar to retrieve her wineglass. She froze when she realized she'd left the newspaper clipping on the counter. She glanced back at Brant, hoping he wouldn't notice. But it was too late. He'd already followed her to the bar.

Valerie's fingers itched to snatch up the article before he could see it, but that would only call attention to it, add importance to it. So she did nothing but sip her wine and watch Brant's reaction.

He studied the picture for a moment, then slowly his gaze lifted. "I remember this picture," he said. "It was shown all over the country after the arrest. My father has a framed copy in his office at the house."

The thought made Valerie's skin crawl. "The press went crazy with that story. 'The big, strong policeman who caught little Adam Kingsley's kidnapper taking the time to comfort the suspect's daughter.' The public loved it."

"I remember seeing that little girl on the news," Brant said. "I thought she looked so lost and alone that night, standing there watching her father being taken away. But a tiny part of me envied her."

Valerie gaped at him in shock. "*Envied* her? Why?"

"Because she'd managed to do something I never could. She got my father's attention." Brant glanced away, as if suddenly realizing how much of himself he'd revealed. He shrugged. "Kids sometimes get stupid notions."

Valerie didn't quite know what to say. Suddenly she didn't know how to deal with the emotions rushing through her. She felt compassion for Brant Colter because she knew, instinctively, that it hadn't been easy being Judd Colter's son; and she felt guilty for not telling him who she really was.

But how could she tell him the truth? Who would believe her if they knew who she really was?

Brant certainly wouldn't. Not when his own father's reputation depended on her integrity.

He frowned, staring down at the picture. "God knows, my father has his faults. But what you're asking me to believe about him, about the others... I've known them all my life. They're basically good men, good cops. I've followed in their footsteps. Now you're asking me to believe that the three men who were responsible for my wanting to become a cop planted evidence to incriminate an innocent man. You're asking me to believe they conspired to send him to prison." He took a deep breath, lifting his gaze to hers. "That's a lot to swallow."

Valerie nodded. Her throat constricted suddenly, unexpectedly. "I know how difficult it is to believe someone close to you could be guilty of a horrible crime, but who else would want to silence me? Who else would be afraid of what I might find out by investigating the Kingsley kidnapping? Who else would stand to lose their reputations if the truth came out?"

If possible, Brant's eyes deepened even more. "Only one other person I can think of."

She looked at him in surprise. "Who?"

"If Cletus Brown is innocent, the real kidnapper is still free. He—or she—would definitely have a vested interest in keeping the truth from coming out."

"Yes, but—"

Brant shrugged. "But what? You've accused my father and my uncle and Captain Rawlins of letting their egos send an innocent man to prison, but you haven't suggested who you think really kidnapped Adam Kingsley. Surely you have a theory on that, as well."

Valerie gazed at him in anger. His attack had been so subtle, she hadn't seen it coming. "I never claimed I could solve the kidnapping," she defended. "All I want to do is prove Cletus Brown's innocence. Someone has threatened my life twice in two days. Even you have to admit I must be on the right track. I must be making someone awfully nervous."

"I don't know *what* to think anymore." He ran his hand through his hair, and moisture glistened in the dark strands. For the first time, Valerie realized it had started to drizzle outside. Somehow the knowledge made her house seem safer, cozier. More intimate.

She couldn't take her eyes off Brant Colter. She wondered again if he had tried to kiss her earlier what her reaction would have been. And if he tried now?

He was an attractive man, no question. The epitome of "tall, dark and handsome." He made Valerie's insides quiver, just looking at him. But he was also a cop and a Colter, and kissing him would seem just a little too much like fraternizing with the enemy.

"Maybe another detective should be assigned to my case," she suggested. "I don't see how you can remain objective, under the circumstances."

His eyes were deep and dark and full of mystery as he straightened from the bar and took her arm. Valerie felt the warmth of his touch all the way to her soul. "Believe me, you don't want me off this case," he said gravely.

Valerie strove for defiance, but could only muster a soft, "Why not?"

He stared down at her. "Because no one wants to find the truth more than I do."

CHAPTER FIVE

VALERIE GLANCED in her rearview mirror as she pulled into the parking lot of the Sunnydale Nursing Home, half expecting to see Brant pull in behind her. But in the hour or so it had taken her to drive here, she'd seen no indication that she had been followed. She wasn't sure if that was good news or bad.

Maybe Brant had taken her suggestion seriously. Maybe he'd decided to remove himself from the case. That thought should have made Valerie breathe easier, but didn't. In spite of herself, she'd believed him last night when he'd said no one wanted the truth more than he.

Things had certainly taken a strange turn, Valerie decided, as she walked into the lobby of the nursing home. Suddenly, she and Brant Colter were after the same thing, albeit for very different reasons.

An aide showed her down the hall to Odell Campbell's room. It was hard to think of the man—a stranger she didn't even remember—as her uncle. But when she walked into the room and saw him slumped in a rocking chair near the window, his vacant eyes staring outside but seeing only God knew what, something welled inside Valerie. It wasn't recognition, exactly; only a faint stirring of some emotion she couldn't quite define.

Other than her father, this man was her only living

relative. There was a bond between them, and it hurt Valerie to see what the disease had done to him.

She crossed the room and knelt beside his rocker. "Hello," she said softly.

There was no response, not so much as a blink, and Valerie glanced up at the aide, who still stood in the doorway. "Poor thing," she said sorrowfully. "He's getting worse every day. I can't remember the last time he spoke."

"Can I have a moment or two alone with him?" Valerie asked.

"Sure. But don't expect miracles," the woman warned, before closing the door.

Valerie knelt silently for a moment, gazing at her uncle's profile. In spite of his age and the toll the disease had taken, she could see a faint resemblance to her mother. The knowledge brought sudden tears to her eyes.

"My name's Valerie," she said softly. "But it used to be Violet. Violet Brown. I'm Grace's daughter."

Was it her imagination, or had his eyes flickered? He didn't turn his head, didn't make any outward movement at all, but Valerie could have sworn his eyes blinked in response.

"Do you remember Grace? She was your sister. She told me once that the two of you were very close as children. You used to take care of her."

Again that tiny flicker. His cracked lips opened, and the sound he emitted was hardly recognizable as human. Valerie's first inclination was to flinch away from him, but compassion stirred inside her. She reached out and placed her hand over his. His skin felt like parchment, dry and thin and very fragile.

"Gracie," he whispered.

Valerie's heart surged. "Yes! Gracie. That's what you always called her. Do you remember her? Do you remember her husband, Cletus?"

Valerie watched his expression closely for any sign that he might have heard her, might have recognized her father's name, but Odell's expression became blank again, his eyes vacant and staring. She began to wonder if she had imagined him whispering her mother's name.

Trying to smother her disappointment, Valerie pulled up a straight-backed chair and sat down beside him. After a moment, she began to talk to him about her mother and father, about what had happened after the Kingsley kidnapping. She talked for at least ten minutes and didn't get one reaction from her uncle.

Finally, she sighed and stood. For a long time, she stared down at him. Then she said softly, "I'm glad I came to see you. I don't know why you did what you did back then, but it seems to me you've paid for it. I forgive you, and I'm sure my father would, too, if he knew."

The cracked lips moved again, but no sound came out. Valerie bent and listened closely.

"Are you trying to tell me something about my father?" she whispered.

"Innocent," the voice croaked. "Innocent."

VALERIE THOUGHT ABOUT what her uncle had said as she walked down the hall toward the lobby. Had he really said "innocent," or had she simply heard what she'd wanted to hear?

The latter seemed more plausible, given his condition. And besides, even if it hadn't been her imagination, a man in the advanced stages of Alzheimer's wouldn't be considered a reliable witness. It would be her word— hearsay—and no court in the country would accept it as evidence.

"Miss Snow?" She turned and saw the aide who had shown her to her uncle's room hurrying down the hall toward her. "I was afraid I'd missed you," she said breathlessly. "I need to ask you something."

Valerie gazed at her curiously. "What is it?"

"Are you related to Mr. Campbell?"

Valerie hesitated. "As I told you earlier, I'm a reporter for a newspaper in Memphis."

"Right," she said. "But if you aren't a relative, I was hoping you might at least know how we could get in touch with his next of kin."

"Why?" Valerie asked evasively. "Is there some problem?"

"No, not really. It's really kind of strange, though. And sad. You see, Mr. Campbell's lawyer admitted him to the nursing home. It seems Mr. Campbell had been living on the streets for years, even before he became ill. Everyone thought he was just another homeless person, but he had money. Quite a bit of it. He just wouldn't use it on himself."

Valerie gazed at her in astonishment. "What do you mean?"

"I mean he wouldn't touch a penny of his savings. He drew up a will years ago, leaving everything to his sister and her daughter. But his lawyer, a Mr. Dickey, hasn't been able to locate either one of them. You'd think they'd want to know about him, wouldn't you? You'd think they'd at least come to see him, poor old soul." The woman's gaze hardened. "I'll bet after he's gone, they'll turn up. Won't be able to claim that inheritance fast enough."

"I'm sorry," Valerie said, reeling from what she had just learned. "I can't help you."

The nurse nodded. "It was just a long shot. Will you be back to see him?"

"I'll try."

Valerie walked outside into brilliant sunlight. Shading her eyes, she crossed the parking lot to her car and got in. Her hand shook when she inserted the key into the ignition, and she sat for a moment, trying to regain her composure.

Her uncle had been on the streets for years, a homeless person living off handouts and garbage, when all along he'd had money in the bank. Money he wouldn't touch.

Money he was leaving to her.

How ironic was that? she thought, feeling slightly sick to her stomach. The money that had been used to buy Odell's testimony, to get him to help send Valerie's father to prison, would be hers the moment her uncle passed away.

SECURITY WAS TIGHT that night for Austin Colter's fund-raiser, the first such event to be held at the Kingsley estate since little Adam Kingsley had been kidnapped. A guard stationed at the gatehouse inspected the guests' invitations before allowing the cars to proceed up the drive, a private road that led back into a deep forest of pines. Around a sharp curve, the drive abruptly gave way to a wide, sloping lawn and manicured gardens adorned with marble statues, colored fountains and giant topiaries.

The house was a redbrick Tudor affair with a gabled roof and hundreds of windows that reflected light like gemstones.

Julian pulled the Mercedes around the curved drive and parked in front of the mansion. An attendant opened the door for Valerie and helped her out, while another climbed behind the wheel. The car sped off, and Julian and Valerie were left standing at the foot of the marble stairs that led to the front entrance.

For a moment, Valerie couldn't move. The pictures she'd seen of the mansion had not prepared her for the reality, for the sheer enormity of the place.

An eerie chill descended over her as she stood staring up at the house. It was brilliantly lit, as it would have been on that night thirty-one years ago. The movers and shakers of the state would have been arriving for Edward Kingsley's fund-raiser, just as they were tonight for Austin Colter. No one would have suspected that in just a few short hours, a terrible tragedy would occur, one with far-reaching consequences.

One that would change lives forever.

Valerie shivered again as her gaze drifted over the row of second-floor windows. She'd read somewhere that the nursery was located at the rear of the house, with a small balcony that overlooked the back gardens. According to newspaper accounts of police testimony given at the trial, it was from this balcony that the kidnapper had gained access to the house. He had somehow scaled the wall, climbed onto the balcony, and entered through the French doors, which had been left unlocked by the nanny.

Little Adam Kingsley had then been taken from his crib—possibly after having been drugged—and somehow lowered to the ground, then spirited away without a trace while two other children—his twin brother and a little girl—slept on in the same room, and the nanny in an adjoining room.

The kidnapping had taken daring and cunning and, it had always been speculated, an accomplice. Possibly someone inside the Kingsley house.

For a while, the police had suspected the nanny, a young woman named Jenny Arpello, who had worked for the Kingsleys only a short time before the kidnapping. But after Valerie's father was arrested, no connection between the two could be made, and Jenny Arpello had eventually been cleared and was now living up north somewhere.

Valerie thought about what Brant had said last night—that if Cletus Brown was innocent, the real kidnapper was still free, and he—or she—could be trying to stop her from finding out the truth.

Valerie's mission took on a new and more ominous reality. Suddenly, she was dealing with more than a police cover-up, more than a few old men who wanted to fiercely guard their reputations. The specter of the kidnapper loomed over her, a man or woman who had once brutally killed. Who would do so again, if cornered.

Was there a connection, she wondered, between the police cover-up and the kidnapper? Was she really dealing with two separate crimes, two separate threats, or just one?

Somehow she had never let herself make that association: that the police—in other words, Judd Colter, Raymond Colter and Hugh Rawlins—had been involved in the kidnapping itself. But what if they had been? That would make them even more desperate to silence her, wouldn't it?

Desperate enough to kill.

Again.

She shuddered at the implication of her thoughts.

"Cold?" Julian casually put an arm around her shoulder, but Valerie quickly pulled away, not wanting him to get the wrong idea.

"Just a little nervous." Julian had expressed a not-so-subtle interest in her before, but Valerie had always been quick to let him know their relationship was—and always would be—nothing more than business. Julian Temple just wasn't her type.

And what is *your type?* she asked herself dryly. How could she possibly know what her type was when she'd never indulged herself in fantasies, never allowed herself to become seriously involved? She had always believed herself to be the daughter of a killer, too tainted to become close to anyone.

But what about now? What if she proved her father's innocence? Might she have a chance then to love and be loved?

And if so, who would *be* her lover? Who would be the man of her dreams?

Unbidden, an image of Brant Colter rose in her mind, and she shivered again, not from fear this time, but from something just as dangerous. Would he be here tonight?

"Here we go," Julian said, offering her his arm. "I wonder if the Grande Dame herself will make an appearance. I can't remember the last time Iris Kingsley appeared in public. She's always been a tough old broad, but there've been rumors for years about her frail health…."

Julian babbled on as they presented their invitations again at the front door, then entered a large, marble-floored foyer. A butler took Valerie's wrap and motioned for them to follow. As they passed along open doorways, she had only a brief impression of the rest of the house—high, vaulted ceilings with skylights; oil paintings and rich tapestries lining darkly paneled walls; glossy wood floors covered with thick, Persian rugs; bronze statuettes adorning marble fireplaces and glass-topped tables; and in one room, a magnificent concert-grand piano.

The butler led them into the ballroom, and here, Valerie had more of a chance to observe her surroundings. She caught her breath. The room was resplendent with dazzling chandeliers, gilt-framed mirrors and huge arrangements of flowers—azaleas and roses and the more exotic hothouse varieties of lily of the valley, orchid and bird-of-paradise—bedecking every corner and crevice of the room and trailing down the gorgeous curved staircase.

A mass of women in glittering dresses and men in somber black tuxedos milled about on the dance floor while an orchestra tuned up on the gallery above the ballroom. It was an impressive gathering, and Valerie felt a little like Cinderella crashing the ball as she and Julian hovered on the fringes.

Like scavengers, she thought uncomfortably.

Julian squeezed her arm. "There's Austin Colter," he said, nodding toward a dark-haired man a few feet away from them. "He's already working the crowd, I see."

Valerie looked in the direction Julian indicated. The man's back was to her, but she could tell that he was talking animatedly to a group of older, distinguished-looking men. He turned suddenly, as if sensing her stare, and Valerie gasped.

For a moment, she thought he was Brant. Then she realized that what she was seeing was a rather remarkable family resemblance. All the Colters looked amazingly alike.

As Austin Colter's gaze met Valerie's, she thought she detected a look of recognition in his dark eyes, a flash of animosity. Then he turned, rather arrogantly, back to the crowd surrounding him and did not look at her again.

But somehow that brief look disturbed Valerie. Somehow she thought she had seen beyond his cool, polished facade and glimpsed a man who might be capable of violence.

The thought left Valerie shaken, for she had seen that same look in Brant's eyes—that same smoldering anger kept so carefully under control. But what would happen if he ever lost control? What would happen if the anger ever erupted? Would either of the Colter cousins be capable of pushing someone in front of a bus? Of shooting someone?

It was a question Valerie didn't want to linger over for too long, because like it or not, she knew she had more than a casual, or even a professional interest in Brant Colter. She didn't want to think the worst of him, and that was a dangerous attitude for a reporter on the trail of a potentially explosive story.

When she looked around, she found that Julian had abandoned her without a word, and she was left alone on the edge of the dance floor as the orchestra struck up a tune. Valerie hastily retreated into a shadowy corner, where she hoped she could observe for a while without being noticed.

Her gaze drifted over the crowd as she tried to picture the scene thirty-one years ago. It wouldn't have been so very different from tonight, she decided. Only the fashions would have changed. The crowd would have been virtually the same—state and local dignitaries, party officials, a judge or two, even a U.S. senator.

The Kingsleys had been steeped in politics for generations, counting among their own two U.S. senators, a secretary of state and several diplomats. Edward had been the first Kingsley in anyone's memory who had run into political trouble. His gubernatorial campaign had been in serious jeopardy back then, primarily because of a hasty second marriage after his first wife died of cancer. The fund-raiser Iris Kingsley had thrown for him the night of the kidnapping had been a desperate bid to rally party support.

But then his son had been taken and later found murdered, and public opinion swayed in Edward's favor. He had been swept into the governor's mansion with a landslide victory, and had served two terms as governor before quietly retiring from politics altogether. Until now.

What had persuaded him out of political retirement to back Austin Colter? Valerie wondered. The two men hardly moved in the same social circles. Their only connection, as far as she could ascertain, was the Kingsley kidnapping.

Funny how that kidnapping had brought such a diverse group of people together. Funny how it was still affecting lives after all these years.

She wondered what the Colters and the Kingsleys

would say if they knew Cletus Brown's daughter was among them tonight. They would be horrified, and would, undoubtedly, have her removed from the premises at once. They might even call her the same vile names she'd been called long ago. They might even say she was tainted with a killer's blood.

Valerie shivered and forced her thoughts away from the past. For a moment, she let the music flow over her, washing away the dark, somber images. As she swayed to the music, her gaze searched the crowd until, with a start, she found the face she'd been looking for all night, but hadn't really expected to see.

The woman in his arms was quietly beautiful, as was the lavender gown she wore. Her hair was light brown, glossy and straight, but the starkness of her hairstyle, the simplicity of her gown did nothing to detract from her beauty.

She was not short, but her thinness made her seem very petite, almost frail, the kind of woman men love to take care of. The kind of woman Valerie had always secretly craved to be but could never quite manage; she'd been hardened by the ways of the world—and by her own determination—at too early an age.

"You needn't worry, you know," said a deep, masculine voice beside her.

Startled, Valerie whirled to find herself face-to-face with a handsome stranger. But he wasn't really a stranger, she thought fleetingly. She'd seen his face in the paper too many times not to know him.

Andrew Kingsley grinned. "Sorry. I didn't mean to startle you. I couldn't help noticing you over here in the corner, all by yourself. I thought you must be hiding from someone."

Valerie took a deep breath, trying to steady her nerves. She couldn't blow this. She'd been trying to get an interview with one of the Kingsleys for weeks now, but both Iris and Edward had adamantly refused to talk to her.

"I'm not hiding," she said. "I was just watching the dancers."

"Yes, I could see that. Your gaze was very intent. You were staring at that man over there." He nodded toward Brant and his beautiful companion. "You had the most interesting look on your face."

"It's not what you think." Valerie felt herself blush. "I mean, I know him…. I recognized him…that's all."

Andrew Kingsley turned back to the crowd, and Valerie did her best to observe him dispassionately. He was tall, a little over six feet, and very well built. His hair was dark, his eyes blue, and there was a tiny, crescent-shaped scar above his right eyebrow.

Valerie wondered if he'd gotten that scar in one of his infamous automobile accidents. According to the tabloids, Andrew Kingsley loved to race fast cars, both on and off the track, and he'd been known to roll more than one expensive automobile in his time.

He was Adam Kingsley's twin brother, and as Valerie stood gazing at his profile, she couldn't help wondering if Adam would have grown up to look like him, if he would have been just as handsome and—from what she'd witnessed so far—as charming as Andrew.

As if reading her thoughts, he turned back and gave her a thoroughly disarming smile. "Judging from the rather pronounced family resemblance, I'd say he must be a Colter."

"Yes, he is," Valerie said, refusing to glance in Brant's

direction. "His name is Brant Colter. He's a police detective."

Andrew's mouth tightened slightly. "That explains it, then."

"Explains what?" Valerie asked curiously.

"How my wife happens to know him."

"Your wife?"

"The woman he's dancing with."

Valerie felt relief flood through her, though she told herself she was crazy for feeling that way.

Almost against her will, her gaze traveled back to the dance floor, where Brant was still holding Andrew Kingsley's wife in his arms. She could sense that Andrew was staring at the couple, also, and for whatever reason, he wasn't at all pleased.

Another woman came up to Brant, this one just as beautiful as Mrs. Kingsley, but more spectacularly so. She looked vaguely familiar, but Valerie couldn't place her. As she stood watching, Brant and Mrs. Kingsley stopped dancing, and the blonde threaded her arm through Brant's in a gesture that was unmistakably possessive.

With an effort, Valerie tore her gaze away and turned back to Andrew Kingsley.

"My wife still has connections with the police department," he was saying, almost to himself. "Her father was killed in the line of duty several years ago."

"I'm sorry," Valerie mumbled, not at all sure Andrew even remembered her presence.

But he acknowledged her sympathy with a slight nod. "I'd hoped she'd severed all ties with…that life, but they still crop up from time to time. I suppose it's only to be expected, especially now, since my family has become associated with Austin Colter's campaign."

"I'm curious about that," Valerie said. "Your family hasn't been active in politics for years. Why now? Why Austin Colter?"

"Our families go back a long way. Austin's father and uncle did something for us once. I suppose my father and my grandmother feel they still owe them a debt of gratitude."

"You're talking about the kidnapping," Valerie said softly, aware she was treading on sensitive ground. Even after so long a time, the kidnapping of his brother was bound to evoke painful emotions in Andrew. "Raymond and Judd Colter were responsible for Cletus Brown's arrest."

Andrew had been watching his wife, a small frown playing between his brows. But he turned now to Valerie. "You know about that?"

She took a deep breath and nodded. "I know a great deal about your brother's kidnapping. My name is Valerie Snow, Mr. Kingsley. I'm a reporter."

The name didn't seem to register at first, and then a slow dawning took hold. Andrew's blue eyes narrowed a bit as he gazed down at her. "So," he said. "The enemy is among us."

"I'm not your enemy," Valerie said. "I would think your family, more than anyone, would want the truth to come out."

"My family thinks the truth has already come out about my brother's kidnapping," Andrew said tightly. "My grandmother and my father are both firmly convinced that the man who murdered my brother is getting his just deserts."

"And what about you?" Valerie asked. "Do you think Cletus Brown is responsible for kidnapping your brother?"

"I've never had any reason to believe otherwise."

For some strange reason, the thought occurred to Valerie that he'd meant to add, "Until now," but had stopped himself in time. She glanced up at him and found that his eyes were once again trained on the dance floor. He seemed more concerned with his wife's dance partner than with the fact that Valerie—"the enemy," as he'd called her—was in his home.

But when he turned back to her, his gaze was clear and alert. He'd dismissed nothing of what she'd been saying. "Would you like to see where it happened?" he asked quietly.

Valerie couldn't have been more shocked by his offer. "The nursery, you mean?"

He nodded.

"Why would you do that?" she asked, knowing that a good reporter would not waste time questioning motives. She should have jumped at the chance the moment he offered. "If you think I'm the enemy, why would you cooperate with me?"

He hesitated, a brief shadow flickering over his handsome features. "I read your article in the *Journal,*" he answered slowly, as if choosing his words with extreme caution. But then, of course, he would be careful about what he said to her. He was a Kingsley, after all. He'd had a great deal of experience in dealing with the press. "You present an interesting theory, Ms. Snow."

Without another word, he turned and walked away, and Valerie, still in shock, hurried after him.

"SO, WHAT'S IT LIKE, living in a place like this?" Brant asked Hope Kingsley. The two of them had known each other for years. They'd grown up in the same neighborhood and attended the same public schools, although Hope had been a few grades behind Brant. Hope's father had been a cop, just like Brant's, which had made them a part of the same big family.

She smiled up at him, but her violet eyes were clouded. "Terrifying. At least it was at first. I'm used to it now, though."

"It's a far cry from the old neighborhood," Brant said, referring to the neat rows of post-World War II homes in midtown where they'd grown up. "How long has it been, anyway?"

"Andrew and I will celebrate our tenth wedding anniversary next month."

Brant whistled. "That long? Doesn't seem possible that…"

She nodded, her eyes suddenly shimmering. "That Dad has been dead for so long? I know."

Hope's father, Dan Sterling, had been killed in the line of duty one night while answering a routine domestic-disturbance call. He'd walked in on a drug deal and had been blown away before he could call for backup.

Sterling had been a veteran officer, one the entire department had admired and respected. Brant could still remember the turnout for his funeral, how broken up his friends and family had been, especially his twenty-year-old daughter, Hope, who had been engaged at that time to one of Brant's friends. Brant and Jake McClain had only been on the street for two years. Dan Sterling's death had hit them both hard, awakened them with a cruel jolt to the realities of police work.

Brant had never really known the details of Hope and Jake's breakup, but he'd always figured it had something to do with her father being killed and Jake being a cop. All Brant knew for sure was that a few months later, Hope had married Andrew Kingsley, and Jake had really been bummed out.

Brant had rarely seen Hope after that, had no idea if she'd been happy in her marriage or not. But she didn't look particularly happy now, he thought, gazing down at her. There was a sadness in her eyes, a longing in her expression that he was pretty sure she wasn't even aware of. If she had been, she would have taken more pains to hide it.

"I saw Jake the other day," he said carefully.

Hope said nothing, but her eyes took on a faraway look he found hard to fathom. "How is he?"

"Don't you see him?" Brant asked in surprise. "Doesn't his father still work for the Kingsleys?"

"Yes, but—"

"You don't associate much with the gardener, I guess."

She looked at him reproachfully. "You know me better than that."

"I thought I did." They stopped dancing as the music ended. He took her elbow and led her from the dance floor. "I didn't think you were the type to dump a guy like—"

"Like Kristin did you?"

"Ouch." Brant winced. "I guess I deserved that."

"Is that why you wouldn't dance with her?" Hope asked coyly. "Are you still holding a grudge, after all these years?"

"I didn't dance with Kristin because I wanted to

dance with you," Brant said with a shrug. It had annoyed the hell out of him, the way his cousin's wife had expected him to leave Hope high and dry on the dance floor and sweep her into his arms, as if it were her due.

But he'd refused and had the satisfaction of seeing Kristin stomp off, her pride and her ego trailing behind her.

Hope looked up at him now, the coyness in her eyes vanishing, replaced once again by a wistfulness that left Brant wondering about her marriage. "You really don't care anymore, do you?" she said softly. "You really are over her."

"It's been a long time, Hope. We've all moved on with our lives. You married Andrew Kingsley, and Kristin married Austin. Maybe that's the way it was meant to be."

"But you never married," Hope said sadly.

He shrugged again. "No. And neither did Jake."

"Don't you ever wonder—" She broke off abruptly, biting her lip.

"What?"

She drew a long breath. "Sometimes it's hard not to think about the old neighborhood, the way we were back then. You and Kristin, me and Jake."

"And don't forget Austin," Brant said dryly. "Always trailing around after us like a stray pup. Always wanting to be part of the gang. I guess he finally got his wish. He got the girl, and some say he's a shoo-in for the United States Congress."

Hope said nothing, but a tiny frown formed between her brows. Brant followed her gaze. She was staring at a couple climbing the staircase. The pair's backs were to the dance floor, but Brant was pretty sure the man was Andrew Kingsley.

He didn't recognize the woman, but she was a knock-out, whoever she was. The simple black gown she wore was subtly seductive, clinging to her curves in a way that made Brant's gaze linger admiringly. Her long, dark hair hung down her bare back like curls of pure silk. She walked with an assurance and grace that made Brant think she must have been born in a place like this.

He watched as she and Andrew Kingsley disappeared around the deep curve in the stairway, then reappeared on the gallery above. With a sharp intake of breath, he saw her face and realized who she was.

Hope glanced at him curiously. "Do you know her?"

His reaction had been anything but subtle. He shrugged casually, but by the look in Hope's violet gaze, he didn't think he could fool her.

"Her name's Valerie Snow. She's a reporter."

Hope's brows lifted in shock. "The one who wrote about the kidnapping? What's she doing here?"

"I have no idea," Brant said, annoyed that her presence had thrown him for such a loop. "I assume she's covering my cousin's campaign."

"I don't think so." Hope looked pensive. "I think she's here because of the kidnapping."

"Maybe," Brant said noncommittally. "Is that your husband she's with?"

Hope nodded, her expression almost painfully empty. "Yes. Leave it to Andrew to find the most attractive woman in the room."

Brant had heard the rumors of Andrew Kingsley's womanizing, but he hadn't given them much credence.

Like his father before him, Andrew's every move was fodder for the press, and Brant figured you could believe maybe half of what was printed. He looked at Hope's face now and thought that perhaps the reports hadn't been exaggerated after all.

"I don't know about that." He swept her with an openly admiring gaze.

Hope smiled. "It's good to see you, Brant. I've missed you. I've missed…you all."

"You don't have to be such a stranger, you know. You still have a lot of friends in the department."

She smiled again and laid her hand on his arm. "Thanks. Will you excuse me now? Iris has just come down. She wasn't feeling well earlier. I really should go check on her."

Brant watched Hope as she made her way toward the entourage that had just entered the ballroom. Iris Kingsley was flanked on one side by her son, Edward, a somber-looking man in his sixties, and on the other by her daughter-in-law, Pamela, who even at her age was still a head-turner in a low-cut scarlet gown.

The reed-thin man with arrow-straight posture standing just behind Pamela would be Jeremy Willows, her son and Edward's stepson, Brant surmised.

Even though the Kingsley kidnapping had affected his life in ways that were still hard to understand, Brant had never given the Kingsleys much thought, had never paid the publicity surrounding them much attention until Valerie Snow had come to town and started asking questions, started writing articles and getting herself into more trouble than she could handle.

Suddenly Brant had become interested in not only the kidnapping, but in the Kingsley family as well, and

he'd started reading everything he could get his hands
on about them.

He knew, for instance, that Pamela was Edward's
second wife, and that he had married her just weeks
after his first wife, his twin sons' mother, had died of
cancer. He knew that Jeremy Willows had grown up to
be an attorney, and that Andrew Kingsley had a pen-
chant for beautiful women and fast cars—evidently a
passion that had not dwindled with marriage.

Brant tried not to think about Valerie being upstairs
with Andrew, alone perhaps, in one of the bedrooms.
He tried not to think of the way she had looked in that
black dress, the way the clinging fabric would slip ef-
fortlessly over her curves, or the way a man's hands—
Andrew Kingsley's hands—would glide over those same
curves.

He tried not to think of Valerie at all. She'd brought
him nothing but trouble with her innuendos and accusations about his father and his uncle and Hugh Rawlins.
He tried not to think about the fact that her life had
been threatened twice, and that the only one standing
between her and the person out to destroy her was Brant
himself.

With an effort, he tore his mind away from Valerie
and concentrated on Iris Kingsley, the matriarch of
the Kingsley clan. Brant had never seen her in person
before. She had to be eighty-five if she was a day, and
she looked every one of her years. She was dressed in an
elaborate white gown that matched the color of her hair.
Diamonds glittered at her wrinkled throat and around
both frail wrists, and Brant thought that the only thing
missing was a tiara.

The Kingsleys had always enjoyed near-royalty

status, and it occurred to him again that the only reason someone like him had been invited into their domain was because of a tragedy thirty-one years ago that had intertwined their two families.

And as if to punctuate that very point, Brant turned to see his mother with his uncle. The two of them were standing very close, heads together, whispering as if they were conspirators.

As his mother glanced up and caught Brant's eye, he thought he saw a look of guilt pass fleetingly across her careworn features.

CHAPTER SIX

IT OCCURRED TO Valerie, as she walked along the second-floor corridors with Andrew Kingsley, that he might have had an ulterior motive for offering to show her the nursery. All the rumors she'd heard about him came rushing back to her, and she couldn't help wondering if his playboy image was well-deserved.

He's married, she tried to reassure herself. *He has a beautiful wife.*

A wife who was downstairs dancing with Brant.

Valerie didn't want to think about that. Her reaction to seeing him with another woman in his arms was too disconcerting, and she needed all her wits about her tonight. The opportunity to be inside the Kingsley mansion, to talk with one of the Kingsleys might never present itself again. Valerie knew she had to take every advantage of the situation.

Besides, she also needed to concentrate on where they were going, and where they had been. The maze of hallways and corridors they'd followed had completely broken down Valerie's sense of direction, and she was very much afraid she would never be able to find her way back to the ballroom alone.

The wing they were in now was on the other side of the house and seemed deserted. She and Andrew Kingsley were completely alone. There was no one about to see them, and no one would be able to hear anything this far away from the main part of the house.

Not even a scream, Valerie thought with a shiver, but she wasn't thinking of herself. She was thinking of that night long ago and little Adam Kingsley's cries for help.

Andrew took her arm and Valerie jumped.

"This way," he said grimly. His expression had darkened since they'd left the ballroom downstairs, and Valerie wondered what he was thinking, what he might be remembering about that night.

He stopped before a set of double oak doors with ornate brass handles.

"The nursery," he said, and gazed at the doors so intently Valerie began to wish she hadn't come up here. Andrew Kingsley was a stranger, after all, and by his own words, considered her the enemy.

But why? Why would the Kingsleys consider her a foe when all she wanted to do was get at the truth?

"No one was allowed inside this room after that night," Andrew said softly, still gazing at the door. "Grandmother saw to that. It was shut off from us children. We were moved to another wing of the house. But Adam's bed is still inside, along with all his toys."

Waiting, Valerie thought, *for the little boy's return.*

A homecoming that was never to be.

Andrew unlocked the double doors and the two of them stepped inside.

Although she had immersed herself in the kidnapping for weeks now, Valerie had never felt closer to the truth than she did at that moment. This room held the secrets she so desperately wanted to uncover. The kidnapper had been in here. Somehow his identity must still be imprinted on the walls, on the drapery, on Adam Kingsley's little bed. If Valerie concentrated hard enough, surely his image would appear.

"There were three of us in here that night," Andrew said, and walked over to stand beside the lone bed. "All the beds were lined up against this wall." He motioned with his right hand, indicating where each of the tiny beds had been placed. "I was here. Adam was next to me on this side, and on the other side, a little girl named Bradlee. Bradlee Fitzgerald. Her parents were old friends of the family. They were at my father's fund-raiser downstairs."

"Go on," Valerie prompted softly, afraid the sound of her voice might somehow break the spell.

"We were restless, the nanny said later. She couldn't get us to settle down. We knew we were missing something, and so we didn't want to go to sleep. It was a warm night, and the French doors were open, though she claimed later she'd closed and locked them before turning in."

The twins had been three years old then. Andrew's memory of that night was extraordinary. Or was he only recounting what he had been told? Sometimes that happened. Sometimes memories turned out not to be memories at all.

Valerie wondered if that was the case with Andrew, but if so, he'd heard the story so many times he sounded completely convincing. He held her enthralled as he spoke, and she had no trouble at all visualizing the scene in her own mind.

She could picture the nursery perfectly as it must have been that night.

Andrew hesitated. "Adam fell asleep first. He was

tired. Pamela had spanked him that morning for mis-behaving at the breakfast table, and he'd fretted about it all day. That's how Adam was. He took everything to heart. He was a very serious little boy."

"You remember him that well?" Valerie asked, trying not to sound intrusive.

He shrugged. "He was my identical twin. I remember everything about him. When he was taken, a part of me was taken, too."

"You still miss him, don't you?"

He lifted his head and stared at her. "No one can understand what it's been like for me all these years. Maybe that's why I do the things I do. The fast cars. The women. The danger. Maybe I'm trying to live life for both of us."

"I think I do understand," Valerie said. "I know what it's like to have your life altered forever at a very young age. I know what it's like to always wonder what might have been."

"He would have been successful, you know. He got the brains, I got the charm." Andrew grinned suddenly, disarmingly, and added, "And the looks."

"You were identical, weren't you?"

He laughed out loud, relieved, it seemed, to have the moment lightened. "Touché." He walked over to the window and stared out. "I didn't believe them when they told me he was dead. I didn't believe he was never coming back. How could I still be alive and Adam dead?"

Valerie said nothing, but watched him turn from the window and walk slowly toward her. He reached inside his shirt collar and withdrew a gold medallion that dangled from a chain. He flipped the medallion to show her that the other side was smooth—like a one-sided coin.

"Adam wore the other side of the coin," he said. "My grandmother gave them to us for our third birthday. We never took them off."

Again Valerie remained silent, sensing something important was about to be revealed.

"After the trial, when Adam's personal effects were returned to us, the medallion was missing."

"Maybe it got lost," Valerie said. "Maybe the chain broke somehow…"

Andrew shook his head. "He was found wearing the same pajamas he'd had on that night. His blanket was in the grave with him, along with a stuffed animal, a little dog, that he always slept with. A signet ring that our mother had given to him was still on his finger. Everything was exactly as it was the night he was taken."

"What are you trying to say?" Valerie asked, not sure she was following his logic.

"I'm saying the medallion was deliberately removed. Maybe the kidnapper planned to send it to us, as proof he had Adam. I don't know. But when Cletus Brown's house was searched, the medallion never turned up."

Valerie's heart began to beat faster. "Are you saying you believe Cletus Brown is innocent?"

Andrew turned to her, his blue eyes deep and dark, so intense they took Valerie's breath away. "I don't know. But for some reason, that medallion has haunted me all these years. I've always thought if I could find it, I'd know once and for all what really happened to Adam. I'd have that one final connection to my brother."

WITH ONE EYE ON the stairs, Brant listened as his uncle hastily explained how Judd hadn't felt up to coming

tonight, and so Raymond had talked Dorothy—
Brant's mother—into accompanying him to Austin's
fundraiser.

"I didn't want to come," Brant's mother said nervously. "Not without your father. But Raymond said
Austin was counting on the entire family being here
for moral support, and I didn't want to let him down.
Mrs. Thurman, next door, agreed to look in on your
father, and so here I am." Her eyes sparkled as she gazed
around the glittering ballroom. "I've never been any-
place like this before, except maybe for the policemen's
ball. And even the Peabody isn't this grand," she said,
referring to the hotel where the policemen's ball was
always held.

Brant had never heard his mother chatter on so, let
alone seen her so excited. Her face was flushed, her eyes
sparkled, and she looked at least ten years younger.

His father's illness had taken a toll on her, but tonight
Dorothy Colter seemed to have put all that behind her.
Brant thought again about that guilty expression on her
face, and wondered just what the hell she and Raymond
had been talking about earlier.

"You belong in a place like this, Dot," Raymond said
fondly. Then, catching himself, he added, "You and Judd
both. I wish he could be here tonight. He and Austin
have always been close."

Closer than he ever was to me, Brant thought,
though, for the life of him, he could never understand
why. Austin had never been a particularly likable or
admirable person, even as a child, but he'd always been
able to wrap both Raymond and Judd around his little
finger.

A born politician, Brant reckoned, spotting his cousin

across the room, pumping hands, working the crowd for all he was worth.

Kristin was at his side, looking radiant and angelic in her gown of pure white, her blond hair piled high atop her head, accentuating her delicate features. She, too, had the crowd eating out of her hand—the successful businesswoman, the polished campaigner, the adoring wife. Perfect in every way except for one fatal flaw.

She could be ruthless as hell.

Brant remembered the night he'd told her of his plans to enter the police academy. He'd just passed the bar and had offers from several law firms he was considering.

Brant had expected resistance from Kristin, had prepared himself for her disappointment, but the temper tantrum she'd thrown had taken him completely by surprise. She'd turned on him, scratching and clawing at his face like a wildcat. If she'd had a gun, Brant had no doubt she would have shot him, so great was her anger. How dared he destroy all her plans?

Brant hadn't thought about that night in years. He'd gotten over Kristin a long time ago, but every once in a while, when he saw her at his cousin's side, her soft, sweet smile lighting up her heart-shaped face, he couldn't help wondering about the woman hidden inside, the woman he'd glimpsed the night she'd broken their engagement.

A woman who had seemed capable of almost anything.

He turned away to find his mother watching him, a sympathetic look in her eyes.

She thinks I'm still in love with Kristin, Brant realized. *They all do. The whole family. But they don't know her like I do. They don't know what a selfish, vindictive woman she really is.*

His mother touched his arm. "I'm going over to talk to Austin. Would you like to come with me?"

"No, thanks," Brant said dryly, although he knew his mother would misconstrue his meaning.

After she'd disappeared in the crowd, Raymond's hand fell on Brant's shoulder. "You don't have to worry about her, you know."

Brant looked at his uncle in surprise. "What do you mean?"

"I'm talking about Judd. Your father suffered a stroke, Brant. He's never going to be the man he was."

"He's getting better all the time," Brant insisted, automatically coming to the defense of a man who'd never shown him the slightest bit of loyalty, other than to remind him from time to time that Brant was a Colter, and Colters always stuck together.

"Let's face reality," Raymond said. "He's my brother, and it hurts me to admit it, but Judd isn't going to be around much longer. You and I both know that. But I want you to know that when the time comes, your mother will be well taken care of. I'll see to that."

"She isn't your responsibility," Brant said, feeling slightly offended but not understanding why.

"I've done well in my life," Raymond continued, as if he hadn't heard Brant's comment. "I've been very fortunate. Sometimes I think the best thing that ever happened to me was taking that bullet in the leg that forced me to leave the department. I never was much of a cop, at least not the way Judd was. Never could measure up to him." A faint bitterness crept into his words, but he shrugged it away. "Hell, we're all cut out for different things in life, I guess. Me? I'm a damned good businessman and a helluva security expert. I've made a good living for myself. Put away a nice little nest egg, more than I'll ever need. I've always thought the world of your mother, Brant. You know that."

Brant's mouth tightened as he listened to his uncle. "Are you asking for her hand?"

Raymond looked shocked. Anger flashed in his eyes, and something that resembled guilt. Brant thought about the way his mother had looked earlier, when she'd found Brant watching them.

Raymond's hand dropped from Brant's shoulder. "That was not called for, son."

I'm not your son, was Brant's first thought. Then he smiled tightly. "You're right. I apologize. But I'm a little uncomfortable with this conversation. I don't know exactly where you're going with it."

"Maybe this isn't the best time to talk," Raymond muttered. He gazed across the room and nodded slightly, as if he were answering someone's signal.

He excused himself suddenly and disappeared among the throng just as Brant saw Valerie and Andrew Kingsley walk down the broad staircase. Both of their faces were carefully devoid of expression.

"ALONE AT LAST," Brant said, and took Valerie's arm to sweep her onto the dance floor.

Valerie looked up, startled by Brant's sudden appearance, and by the way her heart tripped inside her at his nearness. "We're hardly alone," she said lightly. "There must be two hundred people here."

"Really? That's funny. I don't see anyone but you."

Wow, Valerie thought. *Oh, wow.*

Brant Colter, cop, was intimidating enough, but Brant Colter, charmer, was positively devastating. "I almost didn't recognize you," she lied breathlessly. "I don't think I've ever seen a cop in a tuxedo."

"And I don't think I've ever seen a reporter…" His voice trailed away as his gaze slid over her, making her heart beat even faster. "Wear what you're wearing."

"Does that mean you like my dress?" she asked daringly.

"Yeah. Oh, yeah." He maneuvered her onto the dance floor and pulled her into his arms. "Would you like to dance?"

"Do I have a choice?" Valerie asked, wanting to resist the pull of his arms, but finding herself unable to. She slid into his embrace as easily as moonlight gliding over water.

"No, you don't," Brant said, holding her close. So close, Valerie wondered if she would ever be able to breathe again.

She was a tall woman, and her heels made her almost as tall as Brant. Their bodies fit well together, like two pieces of a puzzle that had been separated for too long. Her eyes were almost level with his, their lips only an inch or so apart, and Valerie had the wildest urge to close that small distance. To place her mouth against his and let nature take its course.

"I was surprised to see you here." She hardly recognized the soft, trembling voice as her own. She wondered if Brant noticed the difference in her, if he could feel the rapid beating of her heart against his. "Are you here to offer moral support for your cousin?"

"Hardly. I'm here because I was reminded that we Colters always stick together." He grimaced. "I might ask you the same thing, though. How did you get in here?"

"I came with my boss. Julian Temple."

"The infamous King of Sleaze," Brant said. "How do you stand working for that jerk?"

Valerie shrugged. "He's not so bad. He pretty much gives me free rein."

"And he doesn't worry about those pesky little concepts like ethics and libel and defamation of character. He's quite a guy, your boss."

Valerie felt she needed to come to Julian's defense although, to be honest, it was pretty difficult. She'd seen some of the articles he'd sanctioned in the *Journal*. Her own about the Kingsley kidnapping paled in comparison. "The *Journal* was a failing newspaper before he acquired it," she said. "He's made it into a very successful daily."

"By printing sensationalized stories," Brant replied. "I wouldn't be surprised if he were the one who fired those shots at you last night, just to get a good headline."

Valerie pulled back in shock. The magic of the evening vanished. In the back of her mind, she pictured Julian's glee when she'd told him about having been pushed in front of a bus. His first concern *had* been about possible headlines.

But still...

"You can't be serious," she said.

Brant gazed down at her. "A good cop never rules out anyone as a suspect."

"No one?"

"That's right, Valerie. No one is ruled out as a suspect."

His meaning was clear, and Valerie should have been

relieved, but all she could think about at that moment was the way her name sounded on his lips.

She grew breathless again as they fell silent, their bodies swaying in time to the music.

After a moment, he said, "You and Andrew Kingsley were gone a long time. What was that all about?"

"He showed me the nursery where Adam was kidnapped."

One of Brant's brows rose. "It took that long to show you the nursery?"

Valerie drew back to stare up at him. "What were you doing, timing us?"

He shrugged. "Kingsley has quite a reputation. With women, I mean. I wouldn't want to see you getting in over your head."

"Getting in over my head? In case you haven't noticed, I'm a grown woman, well over twenty-one. I know how to take care of myself. I'm a reporter. I talk to people. That's what I do."

"Fine," he muttered. "Just thought I'd warn you."

"Fine," she said. "Warning duly noted."

He pulled her back into his arms again, and they fell silent once more. It occurred to Valerie that the tone of his comment about Andrew Kingsley had been less like that of a cop, and more like that of a jealous lover.

Her heart almost missed a beat. Could that be possible? Could Brant actually be jealous of Andrew Kingsley because of *her?*

Then that would mean…

She thought about her own reaction when she'd seen him dancing with another woman—Andrew Kingsley's wife. And then later, when the blonde had come up and put her arm through his.

Had the emotion Valerie experienced been jealousy? Or was it a longing to be the woman in Brant Colter's arms? A yearning to have the right to link her arm possessively with his?

Wait a minute, she told herself sternly. This was getting too serious. Way too serious. An attraction was one thing, but these thoughts, these *feelings* went beyond attraction. They bordered on caring, and that was something Valerie could not afford. She couldn't let herself care about anyone or anything except proving her father's innocence.

Brant Colter was the last man on earth she could get involved with. He was a cop, a Colter, the son of the man who had sent her father to prison. He had been on the scene when she'd been pushed in front of a bus, and he'd been there last night, when she'd gotten shot at. There was no reason in the world for her to trust him, except maybe for one.

He'd saved her life last night.

Did that explain her accelerated attraction to him tonight? she wondered uneasily. Did that explain this new closeness between them? This new intimacy?

As if sensing her thoughts, Brant tightened his arms around her, possessively, Valerie thought. Once, that notion would have terrified her, but now it excited her. Thrilled her. Made her feel sexy and vulnerable and… womanly.

They were dancing near the French doors, and in silent accord, they stopped. Brant took her arm to guide her out onto the shadowy, moonlit terrace.

There were people about here, as well. Valerie could hear soft laughter coming from the shadows and strains of music from the ballroom. The moon rose majestically over the garden, crowning the pines with an opalescent glow. A breeze rippled through the leaves, stirring the sweet, heady scent of jasmine.

Valerie and Brant left the terrace, seeking the deeper solace of the garden. Here the moonlight was more patchy, filtering through the lacy filigree of pine boughs overhead. Brant's face was in shadow, making him seem mysterious and dangerous. More alluring than ever.

"You aren't like any cop I've ever known before," she said softly. She caught her breath when he took her hand and pulled her to him.

"Known a lot of cops, have you?"

"A few," she said, and sobered for a moment as the reality of their situation came crashing in on her.

If he only knew, she thought. *If he only knew the cops she'd known.*

His mouth was so close to hers. In a moment, their lips would be touching. They would be kissing, embracing, losing control. And then…

Dear God, what then? Valerie thought desperately. Giving herself to Brant Colter would be a little too much like sleeping with the enemy, but at the moment, it didn't seem to matter. Nothing mattered except the way he looked at her in the dappled moonlight.

"You're not like any reporter I've ever known," he said.

"Known a lot, have you?"

He laughed softly. "A few. No one like you, though. You aren't at all what I expected after reading your article."

"What *did* you expect?"

He shrugged. "Someone more…militant, maybe."

"I can be very militant," she assured him.

He laughed again. "I don't doubt that. That's why you intrigue me so much. You're tough as nails and soft and sexy as hell, all at the same time."

"That's good?"

"That's very, very good," he murmured, just before his lips lowered to hers.

Valerie closed her eyes and waited for his mouth to overpower hers. Waited for him to take charge, as had been her experience in the past. But it never happened.

Instead, his lips rested lightly, so very lightly, against hers, and the tip of his tongue eased out to tease open her mouth. A thrill of excitement began to build inside Valerie until she felt herself responding boldly, passionately, almost desperately, to his whisper-soft kiss.

Suddenly, it was Valerie who took charge. Valerie's mouth that overpowered Brant's. She wrapped her arms around his neck, pulling him to her as her lips opened beneath his, and her tongue plunged inside his mouth. She felt his stunned response, heard the sharp intake of his breath just before his own arms tightened around her, and the kiss deepened.

Excitement exploded inside Valerie. Thrill after thrill washed over her. She would never have believed a kiss, a *kiss,* could do this to her. Make her feel weak and vulnerable, strong and invincible all at the same time. She was tough as nails and sexy as hell, just as Brant had said. And Valerie loved it. She loved every thrilling moment of it.

"My God," Brant whispered, finally breaking the kiss. He pulled back, but he didn't release her. In the filtered moonlight, he looked as shaken as Valerie felt.

She couldn't meet his eyes. In the aftermath of

passion, her loss of control was a little embarrassing. And definitely frightening.

"Maybe we'd better talk about this," Brant said.

"Why?" Valerie tried to bluff. "It was just a kiss."

"It was more than a kiss and you know it. This thing between us—"

Valerie pulled free of his arms. "There is no 'thing' between us. It was just a kiss."

She started to move away, but he took her arm, turned her around to face him. "I'm talking about attraction, Valerie. The dangerous kind. The kind that makes you do crazy things. The kind that makes you forget who and what you are."

Valerie knew exactly what he was talking about. She'd known from the moment she set eyes on him that he could be dangerous, in more ways than one. With just one kiss, he could make her forget who and what she was. And that wouldn't do. It wouldn't do at all.

"We should get back," she said, wrapping her arms around herself and shivering, although the night was warm and balmy, and her skin still felt flushed.

"You can't just ignore it," he said. "It won't go away."

"Then *I* will," she replied, forcing a resolve she wasn't even sure she wanted anymore. "I'm going in."

She looked back expectantly, but Brant didn't move. He stood in the shadows, watching her with the same eyes that had haunted her dreams, reminding her all too profoundly that he was Judd Colter's son.

Valerie knew she would be a fool to let herself forget just exactly what that meant.

"WHERE THE HELL HAVE YOU been?" Julian grabbed her arm and ushered her into a private corner banked with lush flower arrangements. "They're on the move."

"What?" It was hard to focus with Brant's kiss still tingling on her lips. With his warning still ringing in her ears. *You can't just ignore it. It won't go away.*

She would make it go away, Valerie thought. She would do whatever she had to to forget Brant Colter. "Who's on the move?"

Julian nodded. "Take a look."

Valerie followed his gaze and saw Raymond Colter and Hugh Rawlins slipping out of the room. *Two of the unholy triumvirate,* Valerie thought. The only one missing was Judd Colter himself.

"I'm going to follow them," she said. "See what they're up to."

"Good idea," Julian agreed. "Meanwhile, I'll look for Austin. See if I can get a few words from him."

Valerie and Julian split up, and she headed across the room to the hallway down which she'd seen Raymond Colter and Hugh Rawlins disappear. She tiptoed along the corridor, glancing over her shoulder to make sure *she* hadn't been followed.

Double doors at the end of the hallway stood ajar, revealing a dimly lit room that looked like a library or study of some kind. Valerie could smell the pungent aroma of cigar smoke drifting from the interior and hear the faint clink of crystal as liquor was being poured. Then the murmur of voices, all masculine, drifted into the corridor.

"Decent of Kingsley to let us use his study," one voice said more clearly, as if he'd moved closer to the door. Valerie drew back slightly.

"Yeah, well, he doesn't like this business any more than we do," said another. "It's got his mother all upset. She's not in good health, you know."

"She looked like hell tonight," said the first voice. "I can't help remembering the way she used to be. No one dared cross her back then. Not even her own son."

"Oh, well. Those were the days...."

"When is he coming?" demanded a feminine voice that startled Valerie. "He should have been here by now. Do you think something happened?"

"Stop worrying," a third male voice soothed. "He'll be here."

The voices trailed into silence, and Valerie grew impatient. She tried to figure out how many people were inside and had counted at least four—three men and one woman—and that was presuming everyone inside had spoken.

She didn't recognize any of the voices, but she assumed two of them belonged to Raymond Colter and Hugh Rawlins. She had no idea who the woman was, or who the other man was.

Valerie started to press closer to the opening to get a better look, but a noise from inside the study stopped her. Someone entered through another door, probably one that opened from the gardens. Valerie heard the distinct click as the door was drawn closed behind the newcomer.

"Thank God," said the woman. "We were beginning to worry."

"I could use a little of that whiskey," said the newcomer, a man. More clinking crystal ensued, and then, after a few moments, he said, "So what's the plan now? What do you want me to do about the Snow woman?"

At the mention of her name, Valerie gave an involuntary start. She pressed a fist to her mouth to suppress a gasp.

"Wait a minute," said the woman. "Shouldn't we wait for Brant? He's family. He has as much at stake in this as we do."

They were waiting for Brant? He was a part of whatever was about to take place inside that room?

The notion made Valerie shudder. Her every instinct warned her that whatever was being planned in the Kingsley study was something no good cop would ever sanction.

So what did that mean? Brant was a dirty cop?

Why should that thought surprise her? He was a Colter, wasn't he? His own father had sent an innocent man to prison.

A cold knot of dread formed inside Valerie's chest. A part of her wanted to turn from that door and run away as fast as she could. A part of her didn't want to know what was being planned, what role Brant would play in the conspiracy.

But another part of her wouldn't let her run. She knew she was about to find out something important, something potentially devastating. Something that might very well clear her father and save her life. Nothing in the world could make her leave her post outside that door.

Nothing except footsteps coming along the hallway.

The sound alerted Valerie just in the nick of time. Frantically, she looked around, searching for a place to hide. A door stood open across the corridor, and she dashed inside.

BRANT STOOD IN THE shadows for a long time, thinking about Valerie. An exasperating woman if he'd ever met one. How in the hell could she have stood there and denied what was between them after that kiss?

Maybe it hadn't affected her the way it had him, but

Brant thought that it had. Her response had been wild and hungry, almost savage, more than a match for his. He'd felt her tremble in his arms, heard her sighs of pleasure against his mouth. She hadn't been faking. No way.

Why, then, after the kiss had ended, did she do a 180-degree turn? Why had she acted as if she couldn't wait to get away from him? Almost as if she were afraid of him?

Was that possible? he wondered. Had her response, *his* response frightened her?

As she'd pointed out earlier, she was a grown woman, well over twenty-one. Surely she'd experienced passion before.

But in all honesty, Brant couldn't say he'd ever experienced a kiss quite like that himself. He had to admit he'd been taken by surprise. A nice surprise in some ways, but a complicated one in others. She was out to get the three men who had influenced him most in life, and someone was out to get her. Brant was caught in the middle. There was a matter of loyalty to be considered, both family and professional.

But how far was that loyalty supposed to go? Could he, in good conscience, ignore Valerie's accusations?

Maybe he could have disregarded them once, but not now. There was no way he could ignore the threats against her life. No way he could deny the likelihood that someone he knew, someone he cared about, was in up to his neck in attempted murder.

Brant turned to leave the garden, but a movement in the darkness stopped him. At the far end of the house, to the left of the ballroom and terrace, another set of French doors opened into the garden. A shadow slipped from those doors now, moving toward the woods beyond the sloping gardens.

It was odd for someone to be skulking about the Kingsley estate, stranger still that the guards hadn't stopped him. Brant started after him, keeping a safe distance so he wouldn't be spotted.

As Brant followed the shadowy figure into the woods, the smell of damp pine drifted on the breeze. A light rain earlier that morning had deepened the fragrance and softened the soil beneath his feet. He made hardly a sound as he walked through the woods.

The wind picked up suddenly, ruffling the pine boughs overhead. Too late, Brant realized the stealthy sound behind him was not coming from the wind or the trees.

He turned quickly and caught a glimpse of a shadow. Instinctively, Brant put up a hand to deflect the blow, but something caught him at the temple, and he pitched forward into blackness.

CHAPTER SEVEN

VALERIE WAITED FOR the footsteps to pass, then cautiously made her way back into the corridor. Whoever had passed along this way must have alerted the conspirators inside the study, for someone had closed the doors. She pressed her ear against the panel, but no sound penetrated the heavy wood. Knowing she couldn't stay in the hallway forever, she retraced her steps to the ballroom, scanning the crowd for a familiar face. *His* face.

But Brant was nowhere to be seen, and Valerie wondered if he was in the study with the rest of his family. With the group of people who wanted her dead. Or at least silenced.

The thought mocked her as she made her way across the ballroom, to the French doors and to the garden beyond, where only a few moments ago she'd been with Brant. Kissing him. Wanting him.

What was she going to do?

There was no one she could turn to. No one who could help her. Valerie had never felt more alone than she did at that moment, and suddenly the urge to run back to Chicago, beg her boss for her job back, move back into her apartment and resume her old life as if nothing had ever happened, was overwhelming.

She could somehow pretend she'd never read her

mother's diary, had never been convinced beyond a shadow of a doubt that her father was innocent.

She could somehow pretend she'd never met a cop named Brant Colter.

Valerie wanted to run away just as she and her mother had done that night thirty-one years ago, when they'd tried to hide from their past. But an image of her father came to her, and she could see, in her mind, the way he'd looked the night he'd been arrested, the terror and guilt in his eyes as he'd looked down at Valerie and her mother before Judd Colter had led him away.

The terror had been because of what was happening to him. And she knew now that the guilt had been not because he'd kidnapped Adam Kingsley, but because he'd betrayed the woman he loved. Betrayed her the night Adam Kingsley had been kidnapped.

Betrayed her with a woman named Naomi Gillum.

The truth lay with her, Valerie thought. As soon as she talked to Naomi, everything would be out in the open. As soon as she got the woman to come forward, her father would be cleared, and then no one would have a reason to want Valerie dead.

And she would never have to see Brant Colter again.

"BRANT?"

He opened his eyes. He could hear a soft, feminine voice somewhere above him, but he couldn't quite bring her face into focus.

"What happened?" the voice asked anxiously. "Are you all right?"

Everything came back to him then. He lay on the ground outside the Kingsley mansion because someone had hit him on the head. And the concerned voice belonged to Kristin Colter.

His cousin's wife.

The woman he'd once loved.

Brant groaned and sat up, rubbing the side of his head with his hand. "Damn."

"What happened?" Kristin knelt on the ground beside him, her face pale in the moonlight. Her blond hair shone like silver, looking incredibly soft, incredibly touchable as she gazed down at him.

There was a time when Brant had thought her the most beautiful woman in the world. There was a time when he would have done almost anything for her.

"Guess I had a little too much to drink," he muttered, not knowing exactly why he lied, but feeling it necessary to do so.

He struggled to his feet, and she helped him. He was very aware of her hand on his arm as he gazed around. They stood at the edge of the garden, in a patch of broken moonlight. But Brant had entered the woods, following the intruder. Whoever had hit him over the head had dragged him out of the trees and into the garden. But why? So he could be found more easily?

He looked down at his clothes. Bits of mud and pine needles clung to the fabric.

Kristin stared up at him in shock. "*You* have too much to drink? I don't believe it. I've never known you to lose control at all," she said, with a faintly bitter edge in her voice. "What were you really doing in the woods? Your clothes are a mess."

She stepped closer and started to brush the pine needles from his clothing. Brant could smell her perfume in the darkness. It was something light and floral, and he couldn't help comparing it to the scent Valerie had been wearing earlier, a fragrance that was deep, dark and mysterious, like the woman herself.

He'd lost control with her, he thought. Lost it in a big way.

"Brant?"

Kristin squeezed his arm, and he glanced down at her.

"I asked if you were surprised that Austin and I are back together?"

Brant shrugged. "I haven't given it much thought one way or the other."

He saw her frown in the moonlight, and realized he hadn't given her the answer she'd been wanting or expecting.

"Would it surprise you to learn that Austin and I have made a deal with each other?"

"That sounds romantic." Brant tried to ignore the throbbing in his head and wondered how he could politely get rid of her. He had no doubt the intruder was long gone, but it wouldn't hurt to have a look around.

Kristin laughed, her bitterness more open this time. "Romance has nothing to do with it. Winning is the name of the game. Didn't you know that?" She laughed again—a darker, more resolved sound that Brant found oddly disturbing. "What do you think about Austin running for Congress?"

"I wish him luck."

Kristin gazed up at him, her eyes unfathomable in the moonlight. "Bennett's retiring, and the Party wants someone younger and stronger to take his seat, someone without scandal attached to either his name or his career. Governor Chandler has agreed to back Austin, and so has Edward Kingsley. With their support, he can't lose. But if we were to divorce—"

"I get the picture. So what do you get out of the deal?"

Kristin shrugged her bare shoulders, emphasizing the tasteful hint of cleavage displayed by her strapless white gown. "I get to be a congressman's wife. I get to move to Washington. Someday, I may even be the first lady."

And she would like that, Brant thought. She would like that very much. Kristin had always had a fondness for the limelight. She would never have been content as a cop's wife. Her dreams were much grander than that.

"So a deal has been struck," he said. "I guess congratulations are in order."

"I know you don't approve," Kristin said pettishly. "But you never did understand me, Brant. You never understood what was important to me."

"Oh, I think I understood you pretty well." She hadn't been that hard to figure out. What Brant had a difficult time understanding now was how he'd fallen for someone like her in the first place. "So my cousin thinks he's headed for Washington, does he?"

"Everyone does. Like I said, with the Kingsleys behind him, he can't lose. There is just one tiny fly in the ointment, though."

"Just one?"

"This kidnapping thing." She hesitated, then moved slightly away from him, so that she stood in a puddle of moonlight. Her eyes shone like stars as she gazed up at him.

She really was beautiful, Brant thought. She would certainly be an asset to his cousin.

"You've read that terrible article," she said.

Brant shrugged without comment.

"The Colter name is considered a strong asset by the Party. They think the family's history in law enforcement will appeal to a lot of voters who are concerned by the escalating violence in our society. But what that Snow woman wrote—all those lies about your father and about Raymond and Hugh Rawlins—make them all sound like criminals. If she keeps on, she could cause a lot of trouble for Austin," Kristin said. Then added more softly, "And for me."

Brant's patience was wearing thin. "So what is all this leading up to, Kristin? Are you suggesting I do something about Valerie Snow?"

"Someone has to. You're family, Brant. You're a Colter. We all stick together, don't we?"

"What do you want me to do, shoot her?"

He'd said it facetiously, but Kristin looked slightly shocked by his suggestion. Shocked, but not horrified. "I wasn't thinking of anything quite that drastic. I thought maybe you could talk to her."

"And say what?"

"Tell her to stop."

Brant laughed in spite of himself. Tell Valerie to stop? Yeah, right. "Have you ever heard of something called freedom of the press?"

"Yes, but what about slander?" Kristin countered. "What about libel and defamation of character?"

"You could make a case," Brant agreed. "But do you want to call more attention to her accusations? The *Journal* has a reputation for sensationalized reporting. No one's going to take her seriously unless she comes up with some pretty convincing facts. So far, all she's done is speculate."

"You think it'll all die down?" Kristin asked hopefully.

He might have thought so once. But now Brant didn't know what to think. Someone had set out to either harm Valerie or to frighten her, and now it seemed likely that that same person, or at least someone connected, had hit him over the head to keep from being seen tonight.

"I know you'll do what you can," Kristin said. She smiled sweetly in the moonlight, looking like an angel, but her light blue eyes reflected a determination that seemed almost deadly.

IT WAS LATE BY THE TIME Brant finally left the Kingsley estate, but instead of heading back to his apartment, on impulse he drove into midtown, to the old neighborhood where he had grown up, where his parents still lived.

A light shone inside the house and a Lincoln sat in the driveway. Raymond's car.

Brant frowned as he pulled his own car to the curb and parked in front of the house. He sat staring at the meticulous lawn, the well-tended flower beds, the concrete birdbath that he and Austin had once used for target practice with their BB guns.

His mother had been livid that day—one of the few times Brant had ever seen her lose her temper. Most of the time she remained extraordinarily calm. A soothing voice of reason in his years of rebellion against his father's indifference, his sometimes-overwhelming personality.

But Brant's mother had always been there to support him in whatever he wanted to do. He realized now that in recent years, he hadn't been as supportive of her as he might have been. He hadn't kept in touch as he should have, and it struck him, with something of a shock, that he didn't really know his mother anymore. Maybe he never had.

He certainly hadn't realized that she and Raymond had gotten so close since his father's stroke. Brant supposed it was only natural that she would turn to Raymond for support. He was a lot like his brother in many ways, but Judd was the older and the stronger of the two, in both personality and physical stature. He'd always been the head of the family, the protector, but now, since his stroke, Raymond had stepped into the role.

Despite his own problems with his father, Brant wasn't so sure he welcomed the change.

He got out of the car and walked across the yard to the porch. As he climbed the stairs, the door opened and Raymond stepped out.

"Brant! What are you doing here?"

"Just thought I'd drop by and see my mother," he said, in a tone that was slightly challenging.

He heard his mother's voice behind Raymond. "Brant? Is that you?"

Brant pushed past Raymond and stepped inside the small foyer. "I just wanted to make sure you got home all right."

She looked perplexed by this sudden attention. "Well, of course, I did. Raymond drove me home. He was just saying good-night."

Brant turned to his uncle. "Don't let me keep you."

"Brant!" His mother sounded shocked by his curtness.

Brant shrugged. "Sorry. Didn't mean to sound so

rude. But it *is* getting late. I'm sure you want to get home."

Raymond nodded, but his mouth tightened almost imperceptibly. "The boy's right, Dot. I need to be shoving off. I'll drop by tomorrow to see if you need anything. You and Judd."

Brant's mother smiled. "Thanks, Raymond. We appreciate everything you've done for us."

Just what the hell have you done? Brant wondered.

He closed the door behind his uncle, then turned to his mother expectantly.

She gave him a reproachful look. "Why were you so rude to Raymond, Brant? You know how much he's done for us since your father's stroke."

"No one asked him to come around throwing his money in our faces."

"Brant!"

"Don't think he isn't enjoying this, Mother. After all these years, he's finally getting to play the big shot."

His mother looked at him sadly. "This isn't like you, Brant. What's gotten into you? What's happened between you and Raymond?"

"Nothing. I rarely see him."

"So why the attitude? Is it because of Austin? Your troubles with Kristin?"

Brant sighed. "I'm just in a bad mood, okay? I didn't come over here to argue with you, Mother. I really did want to make sure you'd gotten home all right."

She smiled wistfully, and Brant noticed how fragile she looked, how indescribably weary she seemed.

"I'm fine, Brant, really. You don't need to worry. I was just about to look in on your father, and then I'm going to bed."

"Why don't you go on up? I'll check on Dad, then let myself out." When she started to protest, Brant said, "Go on. I'd like to do this for you."

She reached up and patted his cheek. "You're a good son, Brant. Your father is very proud of you. You know that, don't you?"

"Yeah. I know that," he said, to humor her.

After she went upstairs, Brant walked down the hallway to the downstairs bedroom his father had occupied since the stroke. The light was off, but the curtains were open and moonlight filtered into the room, casting a surreal glow on his father's face.

He'd lost a lot of weight since his illness, and the shadows and angles that slanted across his features gave him an almost-skeletal appearance.

Shaken, Brant crossed the room to his father's bedside and stood staring down at him. They'd never been close—more like adversaries than father and son—and Brant felt the gulf between them more strongly now than ever. He'd heard about the exploits of Judd Colter, the legendary cop, all of his life, but Brant suddenly realized that he knew very little about his father, the man.

Brant turned away from the bed, and as he did so, something on the floor caught his eye. His mother had always kept their home spotless. She had a real thing for cleanliness. The bits of caked mud on the floor would have driven her crazy if she'd seen them.

As Brant knelt, he saw more mud near the sliding glass door that led outside. The tiny clumps blazed a trail straight to his father's bedside.

Raising the blanket that draped over the side, Brant

peered under the bed. A pair of shoes had been shoved out of sight, the soles of which were lightly caked with mud and pine needles.

CHAPTER EIGHT

DUSK HAD FALLEN the next day by the time Valerie checked into the Hotel Royale in New Orleans, dumped her luggage in her room, and then headed back out. The streets were crowded, but not as heavily as they would be later. The French Quarter would come alive after dark, and Valerie knew that it would not be wise to be caught there alone. She'd never been to New Orleans, but she'd heard stories from some of her friends who had.

As a reporter, however, she'd been in tough situations before. She knew how to take care of herself, and her innate sense of urgency wouldn't allow her to sit around in the safety of her room and wait for morning. She would go crazy, and besides, if she called first, Naomi Gillum, aka Marie LaPierre, might not agree to see her.

Valerie decided the best course of action would be to drop in on the woman unannounced. Surprise her. Give her no opportunity to run.

But what if she didn't live at the same address anymore? What if Harry Blackman had gotten the wrong woman? Or what if Naomi had gotten wind of Valerie's investigation and moved on? Changed her name so that locating her again would be next to impossible? What then?

Valerie didn't want to speculate as to what her next

step would be if that turned out to be the case. She'd counted on finding Naomi Gillum ever since she'd begun her crusade. Ever since she'd found the woman's name in her mother's diary. She wouldn't let herself imagine the worst-case scenario now.

The street was hot and muggy, but a breeze from the river drifted through the oak trees that lined the sidewalk, making the evening bearable. The buildings along the street were old, some of them crumbling, and all had the signature grillwork and tiny balconies for which the Quarter was so famous.

As Valerie walked along, she could hear laughter and music coming from some of the apartments located above stores and restaurants, and the sound, for some reason, made her lonely. New Orleans was a city for lovers, and as Valerie passed several couples strolling arm in arm along the street, she suddenly thought, inexplicably, about Brant.

New Orleans would be his kind of city. It was not unlike Memphis in some ways, except perhaps, for being a shade more worldly. A touch more decadent. But Brant would like that. He would appreciate the city's darker side, because he had one as well, Valerie reflected, shivering a bit as she conjured up an image of his dark hair and black, probing eyes.

She was finding it harder and harder to remember that the two of them were on opposite sides. That because of their fathers, they were natural-born enemies.

She found it harder and harder to forget the way he'd made her blood race when he'd kissed her last night. The way he'd made her heart pound when he'd held her in his arms.

He was right. The attraction between them couldn't

be denied, but Valerie had to try anyway. She reminded herself of what she'd overheard last night in the Kingsley mansion. If Brant was part of the threat to her, just how far would he be willing to go to protect his family, his father? As far as pushing her in front of a bus? Shooting her?

We Colters stick together. His own words rang in her ears, forcing Valerie to accept the reality of the situation. Brant Colter wasn't to be trusted.

She hurried her steps, knowing that the sooner she found Naomi Gillum, the sooner she would have the proof she needed to free her father, and the sooner they could both get back to the semblance of a normal life.

She turned off Royale onto Dumaine and walked a few more blocks. After about twenty minutes or so, she located the address Harry Blackman had given her. Like many of the buildings in the Quarter, the shop was located on the bottom floor with an apartment above it. A balcony jutted over the street and the door was open. Valerie could hear a song, something soft and mournful, playing on the radio inside the apartment.

There was no sign for the shop, no advertisement of any kind, just the street number painted discreetly on the black door. Valerie had never been in anything remotely resembling a voodoo shop, and she experienced a faint prickling of anxiety as she twisted the doorknob and stepped inside.

The shop was so dimly lit that she thought for a moment it might be closed and the owner had neglected to lock up. But then she realized the dusky interior was intentional. Part of the ambience. Candles burned in wall sconces and in holders on the counter, and the scent of sandalwood and frangipani permeated the air.

The shelves behind the counter were lined with yet more candles, in all sizes and colors, along with an assortment of strange-looking roots and herbs bottled in colored liquid.

Another shelf contained brass incense burners, and yet another, straw dolls. Voodoo dolls, Valerie realized, and the candles and herbs were standard fare for the voodoo practitioner.

No one was about, but a beaded curtain covering a doorway that led to the back fluttered briefly, as if someone had been peering out.

Alarm snaked through Valerie. Ever since she'd arrived in New Orleans, she'd had the feeling she was being watched. She'd told herself she was being foolish. No one knew she was here except Julian. She hadn't told another living soul, but in a voodoo shop, that knowledge was hardly comforting.

Taking a deep breath to steady her nerves, Valerie stepped up to the counter and rang a small, brass bell. She kept her eyes on the curtain at the rear of the shop, and within moments, a hand with scarlet-painted nails and ornate silver rings parted the beads. A woman stepped through.

She looked to be about sixty, tall and very thin. Her hair was dyed coal black, as were the fine brows that arched over faded blue eyes. She was heavily made up, with dark blue eye shadow and ruby lipstick that seeped into the deep crevices surrounding her mouth. Tiny silver snakes dangled from her earlobes, and the black silk caftan she wore gave her the illusion of floating as she glided through the beads.

"How may I help you?" she inquired in a deep,

raspy voice that attested to years and years of cigarette smoking.

"I'm looking for Marie LaPierre."

"You've found her." The woman smiled mysteriously as she made a sweeping gesture with both hands. "Do you wish a Tarot-card reading? A gris-gris to ward off bad luck? A love potion, perhaps?" she added with a sly grin as she took in Valerie's slim form.

Valerie suppressed another shiver. She had to give the woman credit. Marie LaPierre knew how to put on a show. But what about Naomi Gillum? "I want to talk to you about Cletus Brown."

An exploding bomb could not have shattered the quiet more dramatically. Fear flashed in the woman's eyes before she quickly buried the emotion behind indifference. She picked up a crystal from the counter and began to polish the stone. "I don't know anyone by that name. I'm afraid you have the wrong shop. Now, if you'll excuse me, I was just about to close for the evening."

Not exactly true, Valerie thought. A sign at the counter advertised Tarot-card readings twenty-four hours a day. It was clear the woman wanted to get rid of her. "I've waited a long time to meet you, Miss Gillum."

The crystal crashed to the floor. There was no masking the fear in the woman's eyes now. "Who are you?" she whispered.

"My name is Valerie Snow. I'm a reporter with the *Memphis Journal,* and I'm doing a series of articles on the Kingsley kidnapping."

Naomi Gillum seemed to age twenty years before Valerie's eyes. The lines in her face deepened against the blanched skin, and her body slumped forward, as if the weight of the world suddenly rested on her frail shoulders. She no longer looked mysterious and intriguing. Before Valerie's eyes, Marie LaPierre vanished, and the woman who emerged was a very old and very frightened Naomi Gillum. Tears glistened in her eyes as she stared up at Valerie.

"Why?" she whispered. "Why now?"

"You, of all people, should know why. Cletus Brown has spent the last thirty-one years of his life in prison for a crime he didn't commit. It's time for the truth to come out."

"Please." The woman clutched a silver crucifix she wore around her neck. "I can't help you. Go away and leave me alone."

Valerie shook her head. "I can't do that. You're the only one who can help me. The only one who can help *him*. I know the truth about the night Adam Kingsley was kidnapped, Miss Gillum."

"Don't call me that," she rasped. "I haven't been Naomi Gillum in a long time."

"You can change your name, but you can't run away from who you are." Valerie knew only too well how the past could come back to haunt you—suddenly, without warning. "The truth always has a way of finding you. I know you were with Cletus Brown the night Adam Kingsley was kidnapped."

"You don't know anything," the woman said bitterly. "You *can't* know."

Valerie felt a flash of anger at the woman's stubbornness. "I know you were the only one who could have cleared him back then. Why didn't you come forward?"

"For reasons you couldn't begin to understand," Naomi said defiantly.

"Why don't you try me? Why don't you tell me about that night? Why don't you tell me why you've let an innocent man sit in prison all these years while the real kidnapper has gone free?"

Naomi's knuckles whitened around the crucifix. "You don't know what you're asking."

She crossed the floor to the front door, no longer floating, but walking with the shuffling steps of a very tired old woman. She pulled down the blind, locked the door and motioned for Valerie to follow her through the beaded curtain.

A narrow, dimly-lit stairway led to the apartment above the shop. The door opened directly into a bedroom, and they walked through to the living area. The room was decorated with red silk piano scarves, fringed lampshades, and yet more candles. French doors opened onto the balcony, and a ceiling fan whirled lazily over head, barely stirring the warm, musty air. The radio Valerie had heard earlier still played softly, and Naomi walked over and snapped it off.

She sat down on the worn velvet sofa and lit up a cigarette, exhaling a cloud of smoke as she motioned to the chair across from her. As Valerie took her seat, she noticed a deck of Tarot cards lying on the coffee table between them.

Following her gaze, Naomi reached forward and picked the top card off the deck.

"Do you believe in the Tarot, Miss Snow?" She tapped ashes into a crystal ashtray. Her hands were steady now. The cigarette seemed to have calmed her nerves, and yet another personality emerged, one that was a cross between the mysterious Marie LaPierre and the very frightened Naomi Gillum. This woman made Valerie extremely uncomfortable.

She moistened her lips. "Not really. I believe one makes his or her own fortune."

One thin brow arched to a sharp peak. "But if we could know the future, wouldn't it be easier to chart our course? Wouldn't it be easier to know which path to follow?" Naomi turned over the card. "*Le Chariot,* reversed, signifies vengeance. Does this card mean anything to you?"

Valerie swallowed uneasily. "No," she said. "And I really didn't come here to have my fortune told. I told you what I want."

Naomi turned over another card. *La Justice.* Even Valerie could interpret the meaning of that card.

This was ridiculous, she thought. It was almost as if the woman had known she was coming and had stacked the deck. But Naomi Gillum couldn't have known about Valerie. No one did. She'd kept her trip secret from everyone but Julian.

To her relief, Naomi didn't comment further. Neither did she turn any more cards. Instead, she sat back against the sofa and took a long drag on her cigarette as she studied Valerie carefully. But her intense scrutiny was almost as unnerving as the cards.

"How did you find out about me?" she finally asked.

Valerie took a deep breath. She'd rehearsed her story countless times in her head. "Cletus Brown's wife kept a diary. I ran across it in my research, and your name was mentioned several times. In fact, she knew all about you and her husband. She knew you'd been with him the night of the kidnapping. Evidently, Cletus confessed to her after he was arrested. He knew that when you came forward, everything would be out in the open, and he wanted to tell his wife about his...indiscretion before she heard about it from someone else. Only, you never did come forward. You disappeared a few days after he was arrested. No one knew what happened to you."

"How did you know where to find me?"

"After I found Grace Brown's diary, I hired a private investigator to track you down."

"As easy as that," Naomi murmured, studying the glowing tip of her cigarette.

"No one else has contacted you in all these years?" Valerie asked skeptically. "I'm not the first reporter to write about this story."

Naomi shrugged her frail shoulders. "No one else knew of my connection to Cletus Brown. As long as I remained silent, no one was interested in me."

Valerie leaned forward. "Why *did* you remain silent?"

"Why did Cletus Brown's wife remain silent?" Naomi challenged. "If she knew about me, why did she never come forward? Why did she not talk to the police?"

"Because she was convinced the local authorities framed her husband, and that her life and her daughter's life would be in danger if she came forward. In her diary, she said she'd received threatening phone calls. She was terrified for her child's safety, and for her husband's. As long as he was in prison, he was safe. But if she talked, if she tried to get him released, he would be killed."

Valerie found that her own hands were shaking now as everything came rushing back to her. The phone calls that had left her mother terrified. Fleeing town in the middle of the night. The years and years of waiting for their past to catch up with them.

She drew another long breath, trying to clear her thoughts. "That was how the police were able to buy Cletus's silence, too. He was told that if he talked, his wife and child would be killed. Besides, who would have believed him anyway? He was a convicted child-killer who would say anything to save his own skin."

"And he's been in prison all these years," Naomi said quietly.

"For a crime he didn't commit." Valerie's voice lowered urgently. "Tell me about that night. Tell me what happened. Please. I have to know."

If Naomi thought Valerie's urgency odd, she didn't comment. She crushed out her cigarette and lit up another. "Cletus and I met in a bar that night. He was down on his luck, couldn't find work, and he and his wife were having problems. He needed someone to talk to, and I was lonely and had a sympathetic ear. One thing led to another." She paused. "It was just a one-night stand. It didn't mean anything. We were supposed to go our separate ways the next morning and never see each other again."

"Did you? See each other again, I mean."

Naomi shook her head. "No. The funny thing is, I can barely remember what he looked like. But I've never had a moment's peace since that night."

She lifted her gaze, and Valerie thought she hadn't seen a more haunted expression since the night she'd looked into her mother's dying eyes.

"Were you threatened, Miss Gillum? Is that why you ran?"

"I knew if I stayed, I'd be killed."

"By whom? Who threatened you?"

Naomi shook her head. "He was never anything more than a voice on the phone. But I believed him. I've never heard such evil in any man's voice."

Judd Colter, Valerie thought, shivering. Who else could it be? "Did you ever tell anyone about that night?"

"There was one man. He came to see me a few days after Cletus was arrested. It was before I got the first threatening phone call. He wanted me to corroborate Cletus's story."

"Who was he?"

"An FBI agent named Denver. James Denver. I don't think he trusted the local police. I don't think he believed Cletus was guilty. He said he was conducting his own investigation, but I don't know whatever became of him, because that night, I got the first phone call, and the next day, I skipped town."

"Did you follow the trial in the papers?"

"No. I tried to block that night from my mind."

"But you couldn't, could you? That night has haunted you all these years, hasn't it?"

Naomi met her gaze. "Why are you doing this? Why are you dredging all this up now?"

"Because Cletus Brown is still in prison. Because I don't want him to die in that place for something he didn't do."

Naomi's faded eyes studied her intently. "Why do you care so much?"

"If I don't care, who will?" Valerie spread her hands in supplication. "Will you help me, Miss Gillum? Will you come forward and make things right?"

"This is not a decision I can make lightly." The fear

Valerie had witnessed earlier settled over the woman's worn features like a death mask. "I'll need time to think."

"Cletus Brown may not have much time," Valerie pressed. "His youth has already been stolen from him. Don't let him die in that terrible place."

She rose to leave, but Naomi said, "Wait." As Valerie watched, she reached forward and flipped over another card. "*La Lune* signifies danger," she said, slipping back into her Marie LaPierre personality. Her voice dropped mysteriously. "Someone wishes you harm. A man."

Valerie's heart accelerated in spite of herself. "Who is he?"

Naomi didn't look up at her. Her hands were busy with the cards. She flipped over another. "*La Roue de Fortune*. Your destiny is tied to him."

Valerie watched, mesmerized, as Naomi revealed a new card. "*La Maison de Dieu*. He will deceive you."

"Who is this man?" Valerie demanded.

Naomi turned over the last card. "*Diable*. The devil."

BRANT WATCHED THE building from the shadows across the street, wondering impatiently what was going on inside. Surely Valerie hadn't come all the way to New Orleans to get her palm read. What the hell was she doing in a voodoo shop?

A shadow moved in front of the window in the apartment upstairs. Brant couldn't be sure, but he thought it was Valerie. For a moment, she stood silhouetted against the light, her slim, womanly form causing a tightening of awareness inside him. She lifted a hand to shove back her luminous cascade of hair, and Brant thought he'd never seen a movement so sensual. So arousing.

Why couldn't he get her out of his head? Why did he think about her night and day? What was it about her that had gotten to him in a way no woman had in years?

Maybe ever.

Maybe never would again.

He cursed softly, forcing his mind back to the business at hand. He hadn't followed Valerie all the way to New Orleans just to lust after her. He wanted to know what she was doing here, what she was after.

And he wanted to make sure she stayed safe.

A shudder of dread swept through him as he thought about last night. Someone had been at the Kingsley mansion who hadn't wanted to be seen. That same someone had cracked Brant over the head in the woods, then dragged him back into the garden.

And there had been mud and pine needles on shoes stuffed under his father's bed.

There had to be a plausible explanation for that, Brant thought. Maybe his father had taken a walk in the backyard before turning in. He'd made quite a lot of progress with his physical therapy in the past several months, but none of the reports had indicated that he was well enough to be traipsing about the Kingsley gardens, or that he was strong enough or agile enough to take out a man half his age. Not to mention his own son.

His father couldn't have been the man in the garden, Brant thought. But who had it been? What had he been up to? And why had none of the guards—all off-duty police officers—seen him?

After a moment, Valerie walked away from the

window and Brant could no longer see her. He stood in the sultry darkness and wondered why she had come all the way to New Orleans to find a woman, a fortune-teller, named Marie LaPierre.

He walked across the street and tried the front door of the shop, but it was bolted. His gaze lifted to the balcony that jutted over the sidewalk where he stood. The window was open, and he could hear soft voices coming from inside the apartment, but he couldn't make out what they were saying.

It would be easy enough to swing himself up to the balcony and listen at the door, but he couldn't guarantee silence. If he were caught, Valerie would know he'd followed her here, and then he wouldn't be able to learn a damn thing.

Entering a narrow alley at the side of the building, Brant found himself in a tiny brick courtyard at the rear. There was a back door to the building, and a metal fire escape that led up to a second-floor window. As he stood gazing up at the window, the light in the apartment went out.

He hurried back around to the front of the building. Within moments, the door to the shop opened, and Valerie stepped out. She looked up and down the street, as if to make sure the coast was clear, and Brant stepped back into the shadows of the building.

Seemingly satisfied, Valerie turned and said something over her shoulder. Then the door closed, and she took off walking down the street, back toward her hotel.

Brant waited until she'd rounded a corner and was out of sight before easing himself out of the shadows. This time when he tried the front door, he found it unlocked. He let himself into the shop and stood gazing around.

"Hello?" he called. "Anyone here?"

There was no answer, but the flames of the candles danced wildly, as if the air had been stirred somewhere inside the building. Brant walked over and parted the beaded curtain, staring down a shadowy hallway. He could see the back door at the end of the corridor and the narrow stairway that led to the apartment. He called out again, but there was still no answer.

He started up the stairs. Something wasn't right, here. His instincts were on full alert.

He drew his gun and knocked on the apartment door.

VALERIE HAD ONLY BEEN walking for a few minutes when she realized she'd left her purse in Naomi's apartment. Not only was the key to her room in her bag, but so were her credit cards and money, and more important, her mother's diary. No way could she wait until morning to retrieve it. If anything happened to that diary, Valerie would never forgive herself. It was her last tie to her mother, but more than that, the diary held proof—precious proof—that her father was innocent.

Valerie turned and retraced her steps. As she rounded a corner, nearing the shop, she saw a man coming toward her in the darkness. A shiver of fear slid up Valerie's spine. For a moment, she considered turning and running in the opposite direction.

Then she scolded herself for being paranoid. The two of them weren't the only ones on the street. There were several people about, and the man was probably just a harmless tourist.

But he seemed to be staring at her so intently. And in spite of the heat, he wore a trench coat. His hands were burrowed deep in his pockets, and a hat was pulled low over his face, obscuring his expression. As they passed each other, Valerie heard him murmur, "Good evening," in a voice that sent more shivers up her spine.

She nodded and hurried on her way, glancing back once when she reached Naomi's door. The man crossed the street and entered an alley. The darkness eagerly swallowed him, and with a sigh of relief, Valerie opened the door and stepped inside the shop.

Something was different, she thought. Somehow the atmosphere had changed since she had been in there a few moments ago. The candles still flickered. The scent of spices still clung to the air, but added to it now was a more subtle fragrance. A scent that seemed both familiar and ominous.

She didn't call out. She wasn't sure why, but suddenly it seemed important that she not make a sound. That she alert no one, not even Naomi, to her presence.

Cautiously, Valerie made her way through the beaded curtain and down the hallway to the stairs. She climbed to the top. The door to the apartment stood ajar, and Valerie pushed it open with the toe of her shoe.

The door swung inward without a sound, and she stepped inside. The apartment lay in darkness, except for the flicker of candlelight in the living room. Following the beacon, Valerie crossed the floor and stood in the doorway.

The candles cast giant shadows across the room, and for a moment, she didn't see the woman lying on the floor, nor the man who knelt over her. Valerie reached for the light switch just as she saw them, but it was too

late. She'd already flipped the switch, and light flooded
the room, giving her presence away.

Naomi Gillum lay on the floor between the sofa and
coffee table, blood gushing from the slit in her throat.

Brant Colter knelt beside her, his hands covered in
blood.

CHAPTER NINE

VALERIE WHIRLED AND RAN. She heard Brant call her name, but she didn't take time to wait. All she knew was that the one woman who could have cleared her father lay dead or dying on the floor, and the man whose own father she might have implicated had blood all over his hands.

Valerie hadn't trusted him to begin with. In spite of her attraction to him, in spite of her reaction to his kiss, she'd known he had a dark side. She'd suspected he had his own secrets to hide, but she'd never wanted to believe him capable of murder. Not even now, in the face of so much evidence against him.

She stumbled down the narrow stairway and fled through the curtain, into the shop. The beads clicked behind her. The flames of the candles danced wildly as she flew across the room and opened the door.

She heard him clambering down the stairs behind her, but she didn't take time to look back. She raced out the door into the darkness, heedless of her direction.

"Valerie!"

He was still behind her, outside now, racing down the street after her. Her feet pounding against the sidewalk, Valerie gasped for breath, unwilling to let herself give up. She was in good shape. She could outrun him. She *could*.

He caught her arm and brought her to an abrupt halt, whirling her around to face him. Valerie looked up into those dark eyes and shivered. Then her gaze fell to his bloodstained hands—hands that were holding her against her will.

"Let me go!" she said wildly. "I'll scream. I'll—"

"I didn't kill her," Brant said sharply, his grip tightening on her arms. "And I'm not going to hurt you."

Valerie wrenched away from him, but for some reason she couldn't begin to understand, she didn't run. She stood facing him, fear clogging her throat, but she didn't move. Instead she stared up at him, seeing the darkness in his eyes, feeling drawn to him in spite of what had happened.

"You were *there,*" she whispered desperately. "I *saw* you. No one else would have had time to come in after I left."

He glared down at her. "Obviously, someone else did come in. It would only take a second, especially if someone was already inside the apartment."

Valerie caught her breath. "Already inside…" Could someone have been in the apartment the entire time she had been there? Had he heard everything she and Naomi had talked about? Had he killed Naomi to keep her silent?

Valerie shook her head, as if trying to clear her dazed thoughts. She had to think rationally. She had to remember that Brant Colter had been the first one to her side the day she'd been shoved in front of a bus. He'd been at Harry Blackman's office when someone had fired shots inside. And now here he was, on the scene of a murder.

He took a step toward her, and Valerie backed away. "Don't come near me," she warned. "Don't touch me."

"For God's sake," he said in exasperation. "You don't really think I killed her, do you? What possible motive could I have? I didn't even know that woman."

"Then what were you doing here?" Valerie challenged. "Why were you following me?"

A look of guilt flashed in his eyes before he glanced back at the shop. "Look," he said. "We have to get back there. I have to call the police."

"You do that," Valerie retorted. "But I'm not going back in there. I'm not going anywhere with you until you explain to me what you're doing here in New Orleans."

"This is ridiculous. How are you going to explain to the police why you fled a murder scene? How do you think that's going to look? You were the last one to see that woman alive."

"That's a lie!" Valerie accused. "She was still alive when I left her. *You* were the last one to see her alive."

"She was dead when I found her. Who do you think the police are going to believe? A fellow officer or... you?"

Valerie gasped, in outrage and fear. It could happen and she knew it. Innocent people went to prison all the time. "What are you trying to pull?" she cried, trying to mask her fear behind anger.

He gazed down at her with those dark, unreadable eyes. Devil eyes. Valerie thought about the last card Naomi had turned over. *Diable.*

A man would deceive her.

A man's whose destiny was tied to hers.

Valerie shivered violently, not wanting to believe

in anything as capricious as Tarot-card readings, but
unable to deny the inevitable. She was tied to Brant
Colter in ways she couldn't begin to understand. In ways
she didn't want to understand.

He saw her shaking, and his voice calmed. "Look,
I'm not trying to pull anything. I'm trying to make you
see how it would look to the authorities if you run. Let's
go back to the shop and talk about this rationally."

"I don't want to go back in there," Valerie said stub-
bornly. She had a feeling that if she walked back into
Naomi's shop with Brant Colter, her life would never
be the same. She wasn't sure if that was good or bad,
but right now, she didn't think she wanted to take the
chance.

"We can't keep doing this," he said.

"Doing what?"

"Pointing the finger at each other. I know you didn't
kill that woman, and deep down, you don't believe I
did, either. Do you?" His gaze locked with hers, and as
badly as she wanted to, Valerie couldn't look away. His
dark eyes held her enthralled, mesmerized, a prisoner
of her own desires.

She wanted him, and she knew it. Even now, with
death and danger so nearby, she wanted him to take her
in his arms, hold her close, whisper to her that everything was going to be all right.

And then later, when she was comforted…when her
fears had all vanished, his whispers would speak of
different things….

"I don't think you killed her," she admitted grudgingly. "But who did?"

"That's what we have to find out." He looked up, his
gaze scouring the street, probing the shadows.

"We?" Valerie asked breathlessly.

His gaze met hers again. "Yes, we. Like it or not, we're in this together, Valerie. We have to cooperate with each other."

Valerie glanced up at him sharply. "What exactly are you proposing?"

He smiled. "Nothing drastic. You're investigating a thirty-one-year-old kidnapping, and I'm investigating attempted murder. Yours. It's possible, probable even, that the two crimes are related."

"I don't get this," Valerie said slowly. "You're tied to that kidnapping in a thousand different ways. I find it very difficult to believe you would be willing to help me pursue an investigation that might end up implicating the people closest to you."

"Or might end up clearing them," he said quietly.

So that was his angle. If she allowed him to help her, he would be able to protect his own interests.

As if reading her thoughts, he said, "You can trust me. I give you my word I won't do anything to impede your investigation."

"What do I get out of it?"

"You get my protection," he said. "You get my expertise. Not to mention my access to police files."

It was like dangling candy in front of a baby. Valerie couldn't resist the lure, even though she recognized a bribe when she saw one. "You could get the file on the Kingsley kidnapping?"

He shrugged. "I don't see why not. Call it an act of good faith on my part. I want the truth as much as you do. But in the meantime, we have work to do here."

Valerie turned her gaze back to the shop. It seemed an eternity that they'd been standing on the street, but in actuality, only a few minutes had passed since she'd seen Brant kneeling over Naomi Gillum's body. Valerie had thought him a killer at that moment, and now, only a short while later, she'd agreed to work with him. To allow him to help her investigate the Kingsley kidnapping.

Was she out of her mind?

VALERIE SAT IN A CHAIR, trying not to squirm, as the Crime Scene Unit pored over every inch of Naomi Gillum's apartment. Two uniforms had answered the call first, followed by a detective named Melmer, a bald, middle-aged man wearing thick wire-rimmed glasses and an ill-fitting gray suit.

He'd spoken with Brant at length, the two of them talking in low tones and glancing at Valerie so often she'd begun to grow nervous. What if Brant was selling her out? How far could she trust this new alliance of theirs?

Valerie shuddered as she watched Naomi Gillum's body, now encased in a black body bag, being carried from the room. Because of her, that poor woman was dead. If Valerie had never come to New Orleans, if she hadn't been seeking the truth about the night Adam Kingsley was kidnapped, in all probability Naomi Gillum would still be alive.

Naomi's earlier prophesy came back to haunt Valerie now. *Someone wishes you harm.* But it was Naomi herself who had been harmed. Killed because she was the one woman who could have cleared Valerie's father.

"Miss Snow?"

She looked up to find Melmer standing in front of

her. From behind the thick glasses, his gray eyes probed her face, looking, she thought, for her weaknesses.

"I've spoken to Sergeant Colter. He tells me you're a reporter out of Memphis. He also tells me you visited Marie LaPierre here in her apartment, just minutes before she was killed."

Valerie nodded, meeting Brant's dark gaze. "Yes, I did. But she was alive when I left her."

"Did you happen to notice the time when you left?"

"No, but it couldn't have been much later than ten. I left my hotel around nine. It probably took me twenty minutes or so to get here, and then our meeting lasted maybe another twenty minutes."

Melmer sat down in a chair facing Valerie and took out a notebook and pen. The action reminded Valerie of the first time she met Brant, when he'd come to question her in the hospital. Had that only been three days ago?

"What did you come to see her about?" Melmer questioned.

"I wanted to interview her for a story I'm working on."

"What story would that be?"

Valerie hesitated. "The Kingsley kidnapping."

Melmer's thick eyebrows soared. "That had to have been, what? Thirty years ago?"

"Thirty-one," Valerie corrected.

"What was Marie LaPierre's connection?"

Again Valerie hesitated. Was it her imagination, or had Brant leaned slightly forward, as if to hear her more clearly? Even though they'd agreed to cooperate with each other, Valerie still felt uneasy sharing her secrets with him. She still wasn't sure how far she was willing to trust him.

However, she had little choice in the matter now. She was the subject of an official police investigation, and if she wanted to eliminate herself as a suspect, she had to come clean. At least as far as her visit here tonight was concerned.

"Marie LaPierre's real name was Naomi Gillum," she explained, avoiding Brant's deep gaze. "She lived in Memphis thirty-one years ago. I had reason to believe she might have been with Cletus Brown the night Adam Kingsley was kidnapped."

Melmer's gaze snapped up. "Cletus Brown. If memory serves, he was convicted for kidnapping and murdering that little boy. He got life in prison."

"That's right," Valerie said.

"Scumbag should have gotten the chair," Melmer said passionately. His gaze turned steely. "You aren't one of those bleeding-heart liberals trying to free the vermin we work our butts off to put behind bars, are you?"

"I'm just after the truth," Valerie carefully replied, not wanting to make another enemy, especially one who, at the moment, had the power to make her life decidedly uncomfortable.

"Yeah, well, that's what they all say, isn't it? The creeps in prison are the poor, misguided victims of society, and the cops are always the bad guys." He looked at her in disgust. "Lady, you aren't apt to make many friends around here, I can tell you."

"So what else is new?" Valerie mumbled.

Brant said, "We're missing the point here, aren't we? A woman was murdered tonight, and there may be a connection to Valerie's investigation."

Melmer glanced up at Brant. *"Colter,"* he said, as if suddenly making the connection. "If memory serves, the cop who busted Cletus Brown was named Colter. Judd Colter. You related?"

"He's my father," Brant said.

Melmer settled in his chair, his gaze going back and forth between Brant and Valerie. "What the hell are the two of you doing down here together?"

"We're not together," Brant said quickly, as if to distance himself from Valerie. She wondered why she resented that so much. "I'm pursuing my own investigation."

"Into the kidnapping?"

"No. There've been two attempts on Miss Snow's life. I'm trying to find the person or persons responsible."

Melmer drew a long, weary breath. "Damn," he said. "I had to be the one who got dragged out on this one. Are you telling me that a fortune-teller got her throat slit tonight because she knew something about a thirty-one-year-old kidnapping and murder, and that someone tried to whack Miss Snow here because she's investigating said crime?"

"I'm saying it's possible," Brant replied.

Melmer's eyes narrowed. "You got any suspects?"

Brant paused, long enough to start Valerie wondering. Was he holding back? Did he know something? She glared up at him, but he avoided her gaze. "I don't have any suspects at the moment, but I'll keep you informed."

"You do that," Melmer advised, turning his attention back to Valerie. "Just a few more questions, and then you'll be free to go. Oh, and by the way, where can I

reach you tonight if I need to? I assume you'll be stay-
ing in town?"

His meaning was not lost on Valerie. Her movements,
at least for the next few hours, would be closely moni-
tored by the New Orleans Police Department. She would
be wise not to leave town suddenly, without telling them.
She would be wise not to do anything that would cast
suspicion upon her, because she had a feeling Melmer
would like nothing better than to have an excuse to
throw her in jail, with the rest of the "vermin" he so
despised.

A LITTLE WHILE LATER, Brant walked her back to her
hotel. Rather than easing the tension between them, their
new association made Valerie even more uncomfortable
around him. Even more aware of him.

In spite of their differing opinions about the kidnapping, in spite of the fact that they were, in some ways,
still working at cross-purposes, the attraction between
them had not lessened. If anything, it was more potent
than ever.

Death and danger had a way of doing that, Valerie
thought. Of charging every moment with overactive
emotions and sensations.

When Brant took her arm to guide her into the elevator at the hotel, Valerie nearly jumped out of her skin.

"Sorry," she mumbled. "Static electricity."

He stared down at her in the elevator. They were alone
and his eyes told her he knew she was lying. He knew
the real reason his touch had affected her so strongly.

This is not going to work, she decided, and then, in
horror, realized she'd spoken the words out loud.

He smiled at her knowingly. "What isn't?"

"We can't possibly work together." She shoved her hair back from her face. "It just won't work."

"Why not?"

"Because," she said eloquently. "It just won't."

He shrugged. "I don't see why not. We both want to find the truth, don't we? And besides, I want to make sure what happened to Naomi Gillum doesn't happen to you."

Valerie cringed. "Thanks."

"You *can* trust me, Valerie."

"Can I?" She thought about the conversation she'd overheard in the Kingsley mansion last evening. She hadn't actually heard the conspirators inside planning her demise, but Valerie couldn't shake the notion that that had been exactly the purpose of the meeting. And she couldn't forget that they'd been waiting for Brant to join them.

Don't trust him, she warned herself. *Use him, but don't trust him.*

She didn't dare look up at him because she knew she would be lost if she did. She knew his deep, dark gaze would swallow her up, and she would have no will of her own. She would not be able to resist him.

He took her chin and lifted her face to his. "Are you afraid of me, Valerie?"

He made her name sound like a caress. Valerie shivered. "No. I'm not afraid of you. I'm not afraid of anything."

"Not even the truth?"

"Why should I be afraid of the truth? Cletus Brown is innocent—"

"I'm not talking about Cletus Brown or my father or

the Kingsley kidnapping. I'm talking about us. About what's happening between us."

"Nothing is happening," Valerie said shakily.

"Liar. And I thought you placed such a high premium on the truth."

"I do. But there is no 'us,' Brant." His name slipped out so easily, almost like a sigh. "There can't be," she whispered.

"Why not?" His hands were on her arms now, holding her in front of him. Valerie didn't think she could have moved away if her life depended on it.

And maybe it did, she thought fleetingly. Her life could very well depend on her keeping her head, on not placing her trust in the wrong people.

Someone wishes you harm. A man. Your destiny is tied to him. He will deceive you.

"We can't do this," she said desperately. "We're enemies. Your father—"

"My father has nothing to do with this." His grip tightened on her arm.

"He has everything to do with it!" Valerie cried before she could stop herself. "You're his son. You look just like him—"

"But I'm *not him*." Brant drew her to him. "Damn it, I'm not him, and this is just between you and me."

Valerie closed her eyes briefly as he folded her into his arms. She drew a deep, ragged breath and looked up at him.

His gaze was so intense, it took her breath away. She could see desire flickering in those black depths, and something else she couldn't define. Something that made her quiver with fear. With desire.

His fingers tunneled through her hair, and then,

with one thumb, he traced the outline of her lips. Their gazes locked for one last time, and then slowly, almost in unison, their eyes drifted closed as his mouth lowered to hers.

The moment his lips touched hers, Valerie knew she was lost. A thousand warning bells rang in her head, but she ignored every last one of them. Nothing seemed to matter at that moment but the way his mouth felt against hers. The way her body melted into his.

Thrill after thrill rushed through her. Her body tingled with awareness, a pure and dazzling sensation. A part of her wished the moment never had to end, so great was its sweetness, while another part of her yearned for something more.

The bell sounded for her floor and the doors slid open. There was no one on the other side, but Valerie jumped back. She touched her fingertips to her lips as she stared up at Brant.

"No," she whispered desperately. "Not again."

He stared down at her strangely, no doubt wondering why a kiss—one simple little kiss—would make her react so strongly.

He had no idea, Valerie thought. No idea what that one kiss meant. Not only had she betrayed herself, but she'd betrayed her father, as well. How could she have forgotten, even for a moment, that Brant was Judd Colter's son? They looked so much alike. The eyes were exactly the same.

Those eyes were still gazing down at her. "Why are you so frightened?" he demanded. "Why do I threaten you so much?"

She shook her head, ready to deny it, but then caught herself, realizing there was no way she could make him understand. Not without telling him the complete truth, and she had no intention of doing that.

"It can't happen again," she said.

The elevator doors started to close, but Brant reached out and pressed the Open button. Together he and Valerie stepped out of the elevator. She started down the hallway, toward her room.

"Wait a minute." He caught up with her and took her arm. "What's going on here?"

"Nothing." To her vast relief, Valerie realized she'd regained her composure, at least outwardly. She shook off his arm. "Look, I agreed to work with you on the investigation, but fringe benefits don't come with the job."

"Was that all that was to you?" Anger flashed in his dark eyes. "A 'fringe benefit'? I thought it was a kiss."

Valerie fished in the purse she'd retrieved from Naomi's apartment for her door key. "We've been through a lot tonight. The murder and everything. I expect we were just reacting to the moment. Our emotions were working overtime." Not to mention their hormones.

"And last night?" He propped one hand against the door frame. "What was that?"

"It was all just a mistake," Valerie said. In spite of her outward calm, her hand trembled as she inserted the key into the lock. She opened her door and glanced back. "It won't happen again."

"Damn straight it won't," Brant retorted. "Not if I'm to be made to feel like a fool every time."

"You don't have to feel like a fool," Valerie said. "It wasn't your fault. We both got carried away."

"That's very generous of you."

Valerie took a deep breath. "I'll see you back in Memphis. Good night," she said awkwardly.

"Good night, Valerie." He looked as if he wanted to say something more, but then changed his mind.

Valerie closed the door and leaned against it for a moment, her eyes closed, her heart pounding in her chest. What had she been thinking, letting him kiss her again? Had she completely forgotten who he was?

That was the most disturbing part. She hadn't forgotten. She'd known exactly who she was kissing, and still, she'd loved it. Still, she'd wanted more.

What was this hold he had on her? How could he make her want the impossible?

Because a relationship with Judd Colter's son was exactly that. Impossible. Crazy. She felt guilty just thinking about him…that way.

His father had put her father in prison. Her mother had died a sad and lonely woman, a desperate woman, because of Judd Colter. How could Valerie think for one minute that she could ever be with Judd Colter's son?

She stripped off her clothes and got ready for bed, but even after she'd turned off the light, it was a very long time before she fell asleep.

BRANT STOOD IN THE shower and let the water pound against his skin. It was cold and bracing—just the thing to take his mind off Valerie Snow and what had or had not almost happened between them earlier.

He couldn't stop thinking about her. He couldn't stop thinking about the way her mouth had felt beneath his, the way her body had responded to his. Just as it had been last night, the chemistry between them had been powerful, consuming, and for a moment, everything had been swept from his mind except his desire for her.

But Valerie Snow was not a woman to lose your head over, much less your heart. For one thing, he knew she wasn't being completely honest with him. She had her secrets, but just what they were, or how they might affect him, Brant had no idea.

An affair with a woman you couldn't trust was never a good idea. Brant had learned his lesson the hard way with Kristin. He'd trusted her, given her his heart and soul, and what had she done? Betrayed him at the first opportunity. Dumped him the moment things didn't go her way.

In the years since his broken engagement, Brant had had relationships with a lot of different women, some more serious than others. But he'd never felt as dangerously out of control with anyone as he did now with Valerie.

What was it about her that intrigued him so much? That drew him like a moth to flame?

He knew he was playing with fire, but hell, wasn't that part of the attraction? Wasn't that part of the allure?

CHAPTER TEN

As soon as Brant got back into town the next day, he drove straight to the building downtown that housed the police department's archives. The officer on duty, Tripioni, a veteran of the department for more than thirty years, was a big brute of a man with thinning red hair and muscle that had gone soft a long time ago.

He looked at Brant as if he were nuts when Brant told him what he wanted. "The Kingsley file? What the hell do you want that for?"

Tripioni was notorious for wanting to know everyone else's business, and most of the time, Brant humored him. But not this time. This time Brant wasn't particularly anxious to feed Tripioni's curiosity because the man was also notorious for talking.

"It's because of that newspaper article, right?"

Brant shrugged, admitting nothing.

Tripioni nodded. He laid a half-eaten bagel on his desk and picked up a cup of coffee. "It's a damn shame, the abuse the department has to take these days. There was a time when we knew how to deal with troublemakers like that reporter. There was a time—"

"Can you get the file for me?" Brant asked impatiently.

Tripioni gave him a sharp look. He took a long sip of his coffee. "There was a time when people knew their

places," he said meaningfully. "People had respect. Not
anymore. You take your old man. Helluva cop. Never
be another like him. They were all good cops—Judd,
Raymond, Hugh Rawlins. They solved the Kingsley
case right under the FBI's nose. Embarrassed the whole
damn Bureau." He snorted. "Feds thought they could
waltz into town and make us look like a bunch of damn
hicks. Our boys showed them. Brought a lot of respect
to the department, I can tell you that. Got us a lot of
attention, both local and national. Made heroes out of
the whole damn lot of us."

Brant refrained from drumming his fingers on Tripioni's desk while he listened to a story he'd heard dozens
of times. Finally Tripioni finished his recitation and
pushed his bulk up from the desk.

"This is a little unorthodox, you know. You should
have filled out a request. That file is restricted."

"Restricted? After thirty-one years?"

Tripioni shrugged. "I don't suppose it could hurt, your
taking a look. You being Judd Colter's boy and all. But
it could take me a while to find it," he warned. "Maybe
you should come back later."

Brant sighed. "No, I'll wait." He had the feeling if
he left, Tripioni might forget all about the file, and then
there would be an even bigger delay.

Forty-five minutes later Tripioni returned with
two bulging expandable folders and several envelopes
marked "Photographs."

"You'll have to sign for them," he said.

Brant scribbled his name, rank, department, date and
time of day on the sign-out sheet, then headed back to
headquarters. He waited until he was seated behind his
own desk before opening the files.

As he sifted through the folders, he noticed immediately that the autopsy report was missing from the file, though it was listed on the property slip.

The envelopes marked "Photographs" contained crime-scene pictures of the nursery and the grounds directly below the balcony where the kidnapper supposedly had gained access to the house, along with pictures of the shallow grave where the body of Adam Kingsley had later been discovered a few miles from the Kingsley estate. But there were no pictures of the boy's body. No autopsy photographs at all. Brant found that not only odd, but downright disturbing.

As he worked his way through the folders, reading the reports, he tried to visualize the scene through the eyes of the technicians. Eventually the picture grew clearer for him.

On the night of June 24, thirty-one years ago, three-year-old Adam Kingsley had been taken from his family's estate while a fund-raiser, much like the one Brant had attended for his cousin two nights ago, took place downstairs. No one saw anything. No one heard anything. No unidentifiable fingerprints had been taken from the nursery or from outside the mansion.

The Kingsleys often used off-duty police officers for security at the mansion, and such was the case that night. But none of the officers reported seeing anything the least bit suspicious.

Just before midnight, the nanny had gone in to check on the twins before going to bed herself in a room adjoining the nursery.

At about three in the morning, when the last of the guests had gone home, Pamela Kingsley, the boys' stepmother, had gone into the nursery, found Adam missing, and alerted the entire household. The off-duty officers still on the scene quickly called in for backup and began scouring the grounds. No sign of the boy or the perpetrator was found.

The next day, Edward Kingsley received the first ransom call. He was told to bring five hundred thousand in unmarked bills to Overton Park Zoo where he was to await further instructions. The police set up an elaborate surveillance, sealing off the entire park. But something went wrong. Somehow signals got crossed, and the kidnapper was able to slip through the net, contact Edward Kingsley and lure him to a more remote area of the park where he was told to leave the money. By the time the police closed in, the kidnapper and the money were long gone.

The media blasted the department for its incompetence, in particular the three detectives heading up the investigation—Judd Colter, Raymond Colter and Hugh Rawlins. To make matters worse, the FBI arrived and took over the case.

But soon after that, Judd Colter got an anonymous tip that led him to Cletus Brown's house, where fifteen thousand dollars of the ransom money was found in the trunk of Brown's car. An arrest was made, witnesses were interviewed—including Brown's brother-in-law— and it was concluded that Brown had means, motive and opportunity. He was officially charged with the kidnapping.

Two months later, another anonymous call led Judd Colter and his team to a shallow grave a few miles from the Kingsley estate and to the badly decomposed body of little Adam Kingsley. That sealed Cletus Brown's fate. There wasn't a jury in the state, maybe the whole country, who would have acquitted him after that.

But where were the photos? Brant wondered as he finished reading through the last of the reports. Had the pictures of the body been disposed of out of deference to the Kingsley family? Perhaps someone feared an unscrupulous reporter might figure out a way to steal the pictures—or buy them—and print them in a tabloid.

How long had the photos of Adam Kingsley's body been missing? And why?

"WHY WOULD SOMEONE remove the pictures from the file?" Valerie asked as she and Brant talked over lunch. She'd flown in from New Orleans that morning—with, if not Melmer's blessing, his reluctant okay—and gone straight to the office.

A message from Brant had already been waiting for her. "Meet me for lunch downtown at the Rendezvous—12:00 p.m. sharp. Urgent." It had been just after ten then, and Valerie had hardly been able to refrain from calling Brant at police headquarters and demanding to know what he'd found out.

But somehow she'd managed to control herself. She didn't want him to think she was too anxious. She didn't want him to conclude that his help was already starting to be invaluable to her. This new alliance was still a bit unnerving, and Valerie wasn't at all sure she completely trusted him. What if he was trying to deliberately mislead her just to throw her off track?

She had to admit, however, this new piece of evidence was fascinating. And Brant had kept his word. He'd gotten access to the Kingsley file.

He spooned sugar into his iced tea. "I don't know why someone would take them. It's damned irregular."

"There must have been something damaging about the photos," Valerie concluded. "Something someone didn't want others to see. Who would have access to the file?"

Brant glanced up. "Authorized personnel only."

"Meaning, it had to have been someone in the police department, right?"

"Not necessarily. Any law enforcement officer in the state is able to come in and access our files, as well as the civilian clerical staff. I'll check the sign-out sheet, but I doubt if that will help much. There's no telling who might have taken those photos."

Maybe not, but Valerie had her suspicions, and she knew Brant did, as well. Why else had he not reported the missing photos to his superiors? Why else had he not gone straight to Hugh Rawlins with the information?

Because he didn't trust Rawlins, that was why. He might not be ready to admit it yet, but Valerie could tell Brant was beginning to have his doubts—not just about Rawlins but about his uncle and his father; about everyone who had been involved in the Kingsley investigation.

She wished she could take pleasure in the fact that a wedge of distrust had been driven between Judd Colter and his son, just as Judd Colter had done to her and her father thirty-one years ago.

But seeing the torment of doubt in Brant's eyes, the growing suspicion that someone he knew, someone he cared about could have been involved in a cover-up, hit too close to home. Valerie knew only too well what he was experiencing. Soon the self-doubt would begin.

But Brant was a grown man. There was no reason to believe he would labor under the same self-loathing she had because of his father's sins. She'd only been five years old when her father had been sent to prison—too young to rationalize that whatever he might have done had nothing to do with her.

Brant wouldn't think that way. He was a cop. He would be able to handle whatever they found out, Valerie told herself; but an uneasiness began to grow inside her.

If she brought down Brant's father, what would Brant think of her? Would he ever be able to forgive her?

AS BRANT SAT ACROSS from Valerie, he found himself growing angry with her. He wasn't sure why, exactly. Maybe it was that flash of triumph he'd seen in her eyes when he'd told her about the missing photographs, and again when he'd admitted that only police personnel would have had access to the files.

She was enjoying this, damn her. She was enjoying the destruction of everything Brant had ever believed in.

He was being unfair and he knew it. She was a reporter hot after a sensational story, and he'd just given her new fodder. The knowledge of the missing photographs, coming as they did right after Naomi Gillum's murder, was intriguing to him, as well. Brant had to admit that even he couldn't let go of the investigation now, no matter where it led him. No matter who got hurt.

And if he were honest with himself, he would have to admit that maybe, just maybe, his anger with her stemmed more from her rejection of him last night than

her reaction to the missing photographs. She was determined to fight the attraction between them, and even
though Brant could rationalize that was probably for the
best, a part of him still didn't like it. A part of him still
wanted her, maybe more now than ever.

For a moment, neither of them said anything. Valerie
toyed with her salad, then glanced up, her gaze intent,
as if she'd just come to some internal resolution. "Brant,
do you know anyone in the FBI?"

"Why do you ask?"

She pushed aside her plate. The food had barely
been touched. "Naomi Gillum told me there was an
FBI officer working on the Kingsley case who came to
see her after Cletus Brown was arrested. She said he
didn't believe Cletus Brown was guilty, that he thought
someone was trying to frame him." Valerie paused. "If
he's still alive, I'd love to talk to him. I'd like to know
why he never came forward with the information about
Naomi. His name was James Denver, and if you can
locate him—"

Brant lifted his brows. "You'll be forever in my
debt?"

Valerie suppressed a smile, glad that his mood seemed
to have lightened. "How about if I just buy your lunch
instead?" She picked up the check before Brant could
grab it.

"I suppose that'll have to do," he muttered. Then, as
he took her elbow, he leaned down and whispered, "For
now."

A FEW PHONE CALLS and a few favors called in gar-
nered the information Brant sought. Special Agent
James Denver had retired from the Bureau with full

benefits five years ago and was living in a small town called Paradise, in northeast Arkansas. When Brant called Valerie with the information, she wanted to leave immediately.

"Wait a minute," he said. "I have other cases I'm working on. I can't just pick up and leave."

"You don't have to," Valerie replied. "I'll go. I'll let you know what he says. I'll even tape the conversation if he's agreeable."

"No way," Brant insisted. "I want to go with you. I have this weekend off. We can drive up on Saturday."

"That's two days away!"

"Have you already forgotten what happened to Naomi Gillum?" he asked bluntly. "I don't want you to go by yourself, Valerie. Promise me you won't."

She hesitated, wanting to be annoyed by his high-handedness, but finding, instead, that she was grateful for his concern. Was it possible that he really cared about her?

Or did he want to see for himself what James Denver had to say? Did he want to make sure the retired FBI agent didn't tell her something Brant and his father didn't want her to know?

You're being paranoid, Valerie scolded herself. What did the man have to do to earn her trust? He'd saved her life, bailed her out of a dicey situation in New Orleans, gotten access to the Kingsley file and now had located James Denver for her. What else could he do to convince her he was on her side?

Valerie took a deep breath. All that was true, of course, but she still couldn't forget who his father was. She still couldn't forget about the conversation she'd overheard at the Kingsley mansion. Brant was a cop *and* a Colter. It appeared that he was going out of his way to help her, but Valerie would be a fool to let down her guard completely.

"All right," she said with reservation. "We'll drive up on Saturday. But if anything happens to Denver in the meantime…"

"What?" Brant said wearily. "You'll hold me responsible?"

"I didn't say that."

"You didn't have to." She heard the resolve in his voice, and maybe a touch of anger. "But no matter what you think, I am on your side, Valerie. I don't know how many times I have to tell you, I want the truth as much as you do."

"I know." But it was what he would do with that truth once they found it that worried Valerie.

CHAPTER ELEVEN

THE TWO DAYS went by faster than Valerie would have imagined. She updated her notes, wrote a piece about Naomi Gillum's death and what her testimony would have meant to Cletus Brown's case, then asked Harry Blackman to find out what he could on the off-duty police officers who had worked security for the Kingsleys the night little Adam had been kidnapped.

Surprisingly, Julian had been out of town when Valerie got back from New Orleans and hadn't yet returned. No one in the office seemed to know where he'd gone off to. Although his absence was a little strange, Valerie hadn't worked for the *Journal* long enough to pay it much mind. She had other things that concerned her more.

Like interviewing James Denver.

Shortly after seven o'clock on Saturday morning, Brant's car pulled into Valerie's driveway. After a short argument over whose car they would take, Brant finally agreed that Valerie's Explorer might do better than his Camaro on the rural roads they would likely encounter.

Then another discussion ensued over who would drive first, and this time Brant prevailed. He knew the fastest way out of the city—or so he claimed—and so Valerie reluctantly handed over the keys.

Within twenty minutes, they were crossing the bridge into Arkansas, where they took Highway 64 heading due west, driving along an endless landscape of rice, cotton and soybean fields. Two hours later, they turned north, taking Highway 167 into Batesville, and from there passing through the quaint-sounding towns of Evening Shade, Horseshoe Bend, and finally, Paradise.

The town was lovely, with tree-lined streets and charming little houses that boasted overflowing flower boxes, pastel-colored shutters and porch swings that swayed in the breeze. They stopped at a gas station to fill up and buy soft drinks, and Brant asked directions to Denver's place. The address he'd been given was a rural route, and so they'd assumed Denver didn't live in the town proper, but somewhere on the outskirts.

The man behind the counter in the gas station took off his John Deere cap, scratched his head, and looked perplexed. "Donny," he said to a man sitting behind the counter in a cane-seated chair that rested on two legs. "Ain't that the guy who bought the old Sheridan place?"

Donny, a younger version of the man behind the counter, shoved back his own cap and let the chair plop forward on all four legs. "Yeah, that's him. Came from up north somewhere. Fishes a lot. Probably find him out on the lake, this time of day."

The man behind the counter nodded his agreement. He drew a little map on the back of a paper sack and handed it to Brant. "Your truck got four-wheel drive?"

"Yes, as a matter of fact it does," Valerie said.

The man spared her a glance, then turned his attention back to Brant. "Them roads out there get pretty rugged this time of year. Supposed to rain later, a real gully-washer. The whole road could go. If you ain't got four-wheel drive, you could get stuck out there for days."

"Thanks for the warning," Brant said. He paid for the drinks and the gas, and he and Valerie left.

"Did you see that?" she grumbled. "They wouldn't even look at me. It was as if I wasn't even there."

"Maybe you intimidated them," Brant teased. "A glamorous big-city girl like you."

She gave him a sour look. "Yeah, right." She hardly looked glamorous today, dressed in jeans, a Northwestern T-shirt and sneakers. Still, as Brant's gaze roamed over her, Valerie felt a little tingle of satisfaction that he obviously approved of her appearance.

She waited until he had turned his attention to his driving, then she secretly gave him a once-over. He was wearing jeans, too, faded and snug, and a work shirt with the sleeves rolled up.

It was strange, she thought pensively. This man had saved her life once. He'd kissed her passionately twice. But she didn't even know what kind of music he listened to, or what kind of books and movies he favored. What did he like to do on his days off?

She tried to tell herself it didn't matter what kind of person he was, because once she found out the truth, once she'd freed her father from prison, she would never see Brant Colter again.

But that knowledge gave her no comfort. Far from it. She found herself wanting to know everything there was to know about him, every mundane detail, so she could save it up and have something to think about in the future, to remember and savor on those cold, lonely nights in Chicago.

Chicago. The place seemed a million miles away. In the back of Valerie's mind, she'd always planned to go back once her mission was over. She'd always thought that she would pick up her old life right where she'd left off, but she realized now that that life was gone. Forever. She couldn't go back, and with something of a shock, it came to her that she didn't want to go back.

Then what do *you want?* she asked herself seriously as they bounced along a gravel road, heading toward the lake.

It was a question she couldn't answer. Didn't dare answer.

JAMES DENVER'S FISHING boat was hardly more than a dark speck on the horizon as Brant and Valerie stood on the wooden dock and waited. The sun had been shining for almost their entire trip, but just as the man at the gas station had predicted, rain clouds gathered in the east. The lake darkened, looking like yards and yards of undulating gray satin.

Valerie shivered as the wind picked up, whipping the reeds in the shallow water near the shore into a frenzy. The lake grew steadily darker, and the cypress knees protruding from the surface took on an ominous appearance, like wrinkled old gnomes rising from their watery lairs.

The speck on the horizon grew larger as James Denver headed his boat back to shore and to safety. The craft bobbed up and down in the churning water, like the cork on the end of a fishing line.

Finally they could hear the engine put-putting over the sound of the wind in the trees and the water lapping at the shore. Within moments, he pulled the boat alongside the wooden dock, and Brant leaned down to help him secure it.

"Much obliged," Denver said as he lifted a string of perch from the boat.

"Nice catch," Brant commented.

"Not bad. I've done worse." Denver climbed from the boat onto the dock. He shoved his fishing hat back on his head, exposing a lock of white hair, and gave them a curious glance. "You folks waiting for me?"

He was tall and thin, with slightly stooped shoulders beneath the plaid shirt he wore. His eyes were blue, light and piercing. Valerie had the impression nothing much got past him.

"I'm Sergeant Brant Colter," Brant said, extending his ID. "Memphis Police Department. And this is Valerie Snow."

Denver's blue eyes narrowed on her. "Have we met?"

"No, never," Valerie replied quickly. "I'm a reporter working on a story about the Kingsley kidnapping."

"The Kingsley kidnapping?" He pinned Valerie with a gaze so penetrating, she thought he must surely be able to read her mind. "That was a long time ago."

Valerie could feel the wooden planks beneath her feet sway, and she grew slightly dizzy. "You were one of the special agents called in on the case," she said.

"That's right." He turned suddenly to Brant. "There was a cop on that case, one of the local boys named Colter. Judd Colter. Any relation?"

"He's my father," Brant said, showing no emotion.

Denver nodded without comment. He stood silently for a moment, then motioned toward the house. "We'd better head on up. The weather's likely to get nasty pretty fast."

He started up the dirt path toward the house, and Valerie and Brant followed. Once they'd climbed the wooden steps to the porch, Denver said, "I'll just put the fish on ice and be right back out."

It seemed to Valerie that he pointedly did not invite them inside, and she wondered if it was because he was hoping to get rid of them quickly. In a few moments, he came back out, minus the hat and rubber boots, having replaced the latter with a pair of well-worn Reeboks. Taking out a pipe and pouch of tobacco, he lit up and sat down in a cane-seated rocker, the only chair on the porch.

Brant perched on the porch railing, and Valerie stood nearby, watching the two men warily and wondering what was going through each of their minds.

Fat raindrops splattered against the tin roof of the porch—a pleasant enough sound any other time, but Valerie found the noise oddly intrusive, as if the weather were trying to drown out what James Denver might have to say.

He took the pipe from his mouth and rocked slightly to and fro. "What, exactly, are you two after?"

"The truth," Valerie said bluntly. "You didn't believe Cletus Brown was guilty. I want to know why you never spoke out."

His calm blue gaze took her measure. "I had no proof," he said, without disputing her claim. "Just a gut feeling that the wrong man had been arrested."

"You had Naomi Gillum's statement," Valerie countered. "You knew she had been with Cletus Brown on the night of the kidnapping. You knew he had an alibi."

Denver's eyes registered a mild surprise as he regarded her thoughtfully. "How did you find out about the Gillum woman?"

"I hired a private investigator to track her down," Valerie replied, not telling him the whole story. "I talked to her a few nights ago in New Orleans, before she was murdered."

His gaze sharpened on her. "Murdered?"

"That's right," Valerie said. "Murdered. But before she was killed, she told me that you had come to see her back then. She said you didn't believe Cletus Brown was guilty, and you were conducting your own investigation and needed her help. But then she started getting threatening phone calls. She got scared and bolted."

"I wondered what happened to her," Denver said quietly. "I figured it was something like that."

"Do you know who might have threatened her?" Valerie asked. She glanced at Brant, who had remained suspiciously quiet for several minutes.

"No," Denver said, though his tone implied that he had his suspicions.

"Do you think it might have been someone in the police department?"

He shrugged. "The locals were under a lot of pressure with that investigation. They'd moved too quickly on the first ransom call, before we had time to get our people in place. And they bungled it, badly. They were taking a beating in the press, both locally and nationally. I was afraid they'd rushed to judgment on Cletus Brown just to save face. And then after the arrest, even after Naomi Gillum came forward, it was too late. To admit they'd made another huge mistake would have been disastrous for morale."

Valerie looked at him in disbelief. "Are you condoning railroading an innocent man just to save face? Just to bolster morale?"

Denver glanced up at her. "I didn't say that. I'm just trying to explain how things were back then."

"You still haven't explained why you never came forward," Valerie said. "What happened to your own investigation?"

"Once Naomi Gillum disappeared, I didn't have much to come forward with. Cletus Brown suddenly had a change of heart and decided to amend his statement. He claimed he was alone on the night of the kidnapping. He didn't have an alibi."

"Because someone got to him, too," Valerie explained. "Someone was threatening his wife and child if he didn't keep quiet about Naomi Gillum."

"Maybe," Denver said. "But there was little I could do after that, except to keep my eyes and ears open. Watch for other inconsistencies in the case."

"And did you find any?"

He hesitated. A frown creased his brow as he brought his pipe up to his mouth and puffed pensively for a moment.

"Were you present at Adam Kingsley's autopsy?" Brant asked abruptly.

Denver didn't seem as surprised by the question as Valerie was. He removed the pipe from his mouth and set it aside, then turned back to Brant. "I suspect you have a reason for asking that question."

Brant nodded. "I recently took a look at the case file. There were no pictures of Adam Kingsley's body at the time of recovery, nor were there any autopsy photos. And the autopsy report was missing, as well."

Denver released a long breath. He looked neither at Brant nor at Valerie, but stared out at the rain-splattered lake. "The autopsy was rushed," he said. "The boy's body was found at around seven o'clock in the evening. The medical examiner performed the autopsy that same night."

"Was the family called in to make an identification?" Brant asked.

Denver shook his head. "Not that I was aware of. The body was badly decomposed. Physical evidence found on the body and in the grave were used to make the identification. The boy was dressed in the same pajamas Adam Kingsley had been wearing the night he was kidnapped. There was also a blanket that the boy always slept with in the grave with him. Given the location of the grave, just two miles away from the Kingsley estate, and the stage of decomposition, it was a foregone conclusion the body was that of Adam Kingsley."

"But what about the autopsy?" Brant asked. "Surely an attempt was made to match fingerprints, blood type and so forth."

"To my knowledge," Denver said slowly, "the autopsy was used to determine cause of death."

Brant looked at him incredulously. "You've got to be kidding. There was never a positive identification made of the body buried in Adam Kingsley's grave?"

The significance of the conversation had been lost on Valerie until that moment. Her mind had been busy assimilating the previous information Denver had given them, but now Brant's last question jolted her with shock. She gazed up at Brant in horror. "Are you saying the *wrong* body may be in that grave?"

"I'm saying it's highly irregular to use clothing as a

positive means of identification. It's not only irregular, it's downright negligent."

"You have to remember how powerful the Kingsleys were back then," Denver said. "Both the local police department and the FBI were coming under heavy fire from the family to release the body as quickly as possible. They were satisfied that Adam had been found."

"But *still*," Valerie insisted, "wouldn't they want to know for sure? If there was a possibility that Adam was still alive, wouldn't they want to know? Wouldn't they want to do everything in their power to find him?"

"Which brings us to another question," Brant said quietly. "If the body recovered wasn't Adam Kingsley's, then someone went to an awful lot of trouble to make it seem as though it was. Why?"

"I can think of one reason," Denver said. "Though it's purely speculation. After the ransom was paid and the boy still wasn't returned to his family, we all pretty much figured he was dead. We'd seen too many cases like it before. All that remained was finding the body. Without it, a lot of questions went unanswered. The case wasn't as cut-and-dried as the police would have wanted it to be. But once the body was discovered, Brown's fate was sealed. Public outrage was such that there wasn't a jury in the country who would have dared bring back anything other than a guilty verdict."

"So Cletus Brown was sent to prison and the case was closed," Valerie said. Anger bubbled inside her, but she knew that she had to remain calm. She couldn't give herself away now. They were getting too close.

"I wonder how difficult it would be to get a court order to exhume Adam Kingsley's body," Brant mused.

"Damned near impossible, would be my guess,"

Denver told them. "First, you'd have to get permission from the family, and given their objections to the autopsy thirty-one years ago, I doubt Iris or Edward would be willing to cooperate now. Which means you'd have to find a judge willing to stick his neck out to sign the order. It won't happen."

"Maybe not," Brant admitted grimly. "But we can at least try."

THANKFULLY, THEY MADE it back to the main highway before the serious rain began to fall. And fall it did, in heavy sheets that all but obliterated visibility. Although she had complete confidence in her own abilities, Valerie was glad that Brant was driving. It gave her an opportunity to think about all they'd just learned rather than having to concentrate on the road.

But her thoughts matched the weather. They were in such turmoil, Valerie found it difficult to make much sense of anything. She stared out the window and tried to imagine what the Kingsleys would say when told the body they'd buried thirty-one years ago might not be Adam's.

"Damn," Brant muttered, drawing Valerie's attention. He was leaning forward, his expression intense as he gazed out the windshield. "I can't see two feet in front of us."

"Maybe we should pull over," Valerie said.

"And where do you suggest we do that? Have you noticed the scenery lately?"

As a matter of fact she hadn't, but Valerie glanced out now, realizing they were on a section of highway that was bordered on the right by a sheer limestone cliff and on the left by a steep embankment that fell away from a narrow, crumbling shoulder.

To make matters worse, the road snaked around the mountain in sharp turns that were breathtaking in normal weather, but in the rain, were nothing short of hair-raising.

"Maybe you should slow down," she said nervously.

"I'm barely crawling as it is." He glanced in his rearview mirror, and his expression grew even more tense. "What does that idiot think he's doing?"

Valerie craned her neck so she could look out the back window. The vehicle itself was barely visible through the rain, but she could see the headlights closing in on them at a rapid pace. The driver was literally flying down the slippery mountainside.

"My God," she whispered. "He must have lost control of his car."

"I don't think so." Brant's mouth tightened in grim determination as his foot came down heavily on the Explorer's accelerator. The powerful V-8 engine responded instantly. The car shot forward, skidding on the wet pavement and drawing a gasp from Valerie.

She whirled back around to face forward, fear tightening in her stomach. "What are you doing?"

"Making sure he doesn't catch us." Brant's gaze shot from the road in front of them to the rearview mirror.

Valerie turned again, shocked to find the vehicle already upon them. It was a truck of some kind, judging by the height of the headlights above the road. The beams loomed over the Explorer, like twin beacons of destruction.

"He's going to ram us," she gasped.

No sooner had the words left her mouth than the Explorer jolted forward after being bumped by the truck behind them. Brant swore under his breath, gripping the steering wheel as the tires skidded on the wet pavement.

"He must be crazy! He'll kill us!" Valerie cried, trying to see through the sheets of rain ahead. Somewhere in front of them was another curve, a bad one, but she couldn't remember exactly where. She hoped Brant could.

"Hold on," he warned, glancing in the rearview mirror. The truck rammed them again, and the Explorer began to slide toward the edge of the embankment. "Damn," he muttered, fighting for control. Valerie felt the small bump as their tires connected with the narrow shoulder.

Then, miraculously, the Explorer gained purchase just in the nick of time, and Brant steered them around the curve at a breathtaking speed.

Valerie glanced behind them. They seemed to have gained some time on the turn. The truck's headlights were not yet visible. She whirled back around, feeling a tiny measure of relief. Then she heard Brant curse again, more viciously this time, as he began to apply the brakes.

Two large boulders, loosened by the downpour, had tumbled down the side of the mountain, coming to rest in the highway—one directly in front of them and the other one in the next lane. Smaller rocks and debris were scattered over both lanes, and as they approached the two boulders, Brant steered a precarious path between them.

Behind them, the truck came tearing around the

curve, so quickly he must not have had time to see the boulders. Over the sound of the rain and the Explorer's powerful engine, Valerie heard the scream of brakes on wet pavement, then the horrific sound of metal crashing into rock. She turned just in time to see the truck careening wildly toward the embankment. Within seconds it disappeared completely over the edge.

"My God," she whispered, shaken by what she had witnessed and by the close call they'd just had.

Brant eased the Explorer to a crawl, and pulled to the side of the road where the shoulder widened slightly. He handed Valerie his cell phone. "Call 911, or the local sheriff's department, the state police—whoever you can find. I'm going back to have a look."

Valerie grabbed his arm. "But he tried to kill us. What if he's still alive?"

"I'll be ready for him," Brant said grimly, checking the clip in his gun. "You wait here."

Her hands trembling, Valerie dialed the phone, but after the call was completed, she found it impossible to wait inside the car. Brant might need help. She pulled a flashlight out of the glove box, then got out of the car, shivering in the rain as she made her way back up the road, to the place where the truck had gone down the embankment.

The force of the collision had sent one of the boulders flying over the edge, and through the rain, Valerie could just make out the path of broken tree limbs and flattened grass where either the truck or the rock or both had gone sailing down into the wet darkness.

She trained her flashlight down the hillside and started downward, slipping and sliding until she finally pinned the mangled truck in her beam. The door hung open on the driver's side, and as she shifted the flashlight, she saw Brant kneeling over something in the wet grass.

She ran toward him. A man lay on his back on the ground, and in an instant, Valerie knew he was dead. Something inside her revolted, and she looked quickly away, trying not to be sick.

Brant rose and took the flashlight from her. She felt his hand on her arm. "You okay?"

She turned to look up at him. The rain had darkened his hair to almost black, and rivers of moisture ran down his face. She trembled uncontrollably. "Do you have any idea who he is?"

"I'm afraid so. His name is Remy Devereaux."

Valerie chanced another look at the body. The man was tall and thin, and his face, beneath the caked blood and dirt, looked sharp and angular, rather like that of a ferret's. She shuddered again and looked away.

"Did you know him?"

Brant shook his head. "He used to be a snitch for the department, but I never used him. By the time I came out of the academy, he'd moved on."

"But your father used him, didn't he?" Valerie asked. "That's how you recognized him."

Brant nodded. "A lot of cops used him. He didn't care who he sold out, and he could be bought for a pretty cheap price."

"Even for murder?"

"Evidently," Brant said grimly.

He trained the flashlight beam on Remy Devereaux's body, and almost reluctantly, Valerie's gaze followed. She took a step forward, frowning. Now that her initial shock was over, a disturbing thought occurred to her.

There was something familiar about him. Something that touched a memory.

"I've seen him before," she said.

Brant glanced at her sharply. "Where?"

"The other night. In New Orleans. As I was going back to Naomi's shop to get my purse, I saw a man on the street walking toward me. I didn't see his face very well. It was dark and he wore a hat pulled down low, but…" She stared at the body. "I think it might have been him."

"Why didn't you tell the police about this man?" Brant demanded.

"I forgot about him. After finding Naomi's body, seeing you with blood on your hands…" Her words trailed off as she glanced up at him. The whole scene took on an almost-surreal atmosphere for Valerie. Two people had been killed because of her investigation. Her life had been threatened, and now Brant's life had been put on the line. The dead man, Remy Devereaux, had been trying to force them off the road. He'd been trying to kill them both. That meant that whoever had hired him was willing to sacrifice Brant in order to keep the truth from coming out.

Could Brant's own father be so cold-blooded?

Valerie thought about the man who had stormed his way into her home all those years ago. A man who had ruthlessly terrorized her family and sent her father to prison.

Yes, she thought. That man would be capable of almost anything.

She looked up at Brant's stoic profile and wondered if he was thinking the same thing.

CHAPTER TWELVE

TWILIGHT HAD FALLEN by the time the local sheriff had finished taking their statements. Rather than slackening, the rain worsened, and with the coming darkness, made travel all the more perilous.

The sheriff warned them there had been reports of other rock and mud slides along the mountain road, and they would be wise to find themselves rooms in town and hole up for the night. By morning, the rain would surely have stopped, and the highway department could get the roads cleared.

Thinking about the close call they'd had earlier, Valerie had to agree. "But what about you?" she asked Brant. "Do you have to get back tonight?"

"No, I have tomorrow off, too. I think the sheriff's right. We'd be better off to wait until morning to start home."

The dispatcher at city hall scribbled down a list of bed-and-breakfasts in town and wished them luck. Evidently they were going to need it, Valerie thought, because the first three places they called on the list were full. On the fourth try, however, they got lucky. The Other Side of Paradise Inn could accommodate Brant and Valerie for the night.

It wasn't until after they'd located the inn and were

signing the register that Valerie realized there was only one room available.

This is too much, she thought. *Like something from a bad movie.*

"You're sure you don't have two rooms?" she asked anxiously.

The owner of the inn, a slender, dark-haired woman named Emily, glanced at her curiously. "I'm afraid not. There's a big craft show this weekend and most of the rooms in town have been booked for weeks. You're lucky I had a last-minute cancellation. But the room has a sofa," she added tactfully. "It's quite comfortable."

"We'll take it," Brant said, signing the register.

Emily showed them to a quaint, cozy room on the second floor, at the end of a long hallway. The decor was decidedly old-fashioned, with a four-poster bed and lace canopy, braided rugs and a rocking chair set near a stone fireplace. Lace-curtained French doors opened onto a small balcony, and a carved wooden door led into a bathroom, complete with a claw-footed bathtub and a pedestal sink.

The sofa Emily had mentioned was also close to the fireplace, and its deep cotton-covered cushions did indeed look quite comfortable, the perfect spot to snuggle up in front of a warm fire.

"The bathroom has plenty of towels," she said. "I'm sure you're anxious to get out of those wet things and have a hot shower. I'll bring you up a couple of bathrobes. Then we can wash and dry your clothes, and they'll be as good as new in a couple of hours." She turned to leave, then thought of something else. "Oh, and I'd probably better warn you that our power is famous for going out in rainstorms. You'll find plenty of candles and matches in the room if you need them."

Then she closed the door behind her, and Brant and Valerie were left alone. An awkwardness settled over the room. For a moment, neither of them said anything. Brant walked around, locating the candles and matches, and Valerie stood at the French doors, peering out into the rainy darkness.

"You want the bathroom first?" he finally asked.

"No, you go ahead," Valerie said. "I'll probably take longer. I'd like to try out that bathtub."

It seemed almost unbearably intimate to be talking about such things with Brant. But it wasn't as if they were talking about taking a bath *together,* Valerie reminded herself, although, come to think of it, the claw-footed tub had seemed big enough to accommodate two people. She'd even noticed candles strategically placed on the porcelain ledge above it. For ambience? she wondered. Or for convenience, in case the power went out suddenly?

There was a time when the latter would have seemed more likely to her, but now Valerie was having a hard time getting a picture out of her head—an image of her and Brant together in that bathtub, with candlelight dancing over bare skin.

"Valerie?"

She turned at the sound of her name. Brant stood in the bathroom doorway, gazing at her quizzically. Obviously he'd said something to her, but she had no idea what.

"I'm sorry, what did you say?"

His gaze intensified on her. "I asked if you were okay.

You seemed as if you were a million miles away just then."

She smiled nervously. "Actually, I wasn't. I was just thinking how good a hot bath is going to feel."

"I'll be quick, then," he said, and closed the door between them.

In a moment, Valerie heard the sound of the shower running, and to block out the visions dancing in her head, she decided to get out of the room and explore the inn. As she headed down the staircase, she met Emily coming back up.

"I was just bringing you up the bathrobes. The dark blue one belongs to my husband. It should fit your... friend quite nicely." She handed the velour robes to Valerie, along with a plastic bag filled with toiletries, including toothpaste and toothbrushes. "If you'll just leave your wet things in the hallway, I'll be along later to collect them."

"This is very good of you," Valerie said. "I'm sure most of your guests don't come in looking like drowned rats."

"You might be surprised who walks in my front door," Emily said with a smile. "If you need anything else, just let me know."

She turned and went back down the stairs, and Valerie retraced her steps to their room. She placed the smaller of the two robes—a white one—on the bed, and hung the other—the dark blue one with a masculine *M* monogrammed on the lapel—on the bathroom doorknob.

After setting the bag of toiletries on the floor just outside the door, where Brant would be sure to find them, Valerie beat another hasty retreat from the room, hoping to allow him ample time to finish his shower and dress.

When she returned, he was standing at the French doors, staring out at the rain. He turned when she entered the room, and Valerie thought he looked ill-at-ease wearing the robe. He was the type of man who would probably have been more comfortable standing there stark naked, she thought, and shivered.

"Bathroom's all yours," he said, not moving from the window.

Valerie nodded. "Good. I can't wait to get out of these wet things."

She gathered up the white robe, then went inside the bathroom and started her bath. In addition to the candles, she also found an assortment of bath salts and oils on the ledge above the tub, and choosing one, sprinkled the water liberally before shimmying out of her clothes and kicking them aside.

Just as a precaution, she decided to light the candles. What if the power went out while she was in the tub? She would be stuck in the dark.

But the candlelight seemed lost in the harsh, overhead lighting, so Valerie flipped off the switch. A soft glow fell over the room, and by this time, a fragrant cloud of honeysuckle rose from the steaming water. With a sigh of pleasure, she lowered herself into the tub.

Why had she never pampered herself like this before? she wondered. Why had she always been in such a hurry, always pushing herself to be more, do more, have more?

Was it because, deep down, she'd never thought she deserved special treatment? Never thought a killer's daughter should be allowed to enjoy the simple pleasures of life?

While she contemplated this sobering thought, a knock sounded on the door. Valerie looked up, startled. "Yes?"

"Emily's come for our clothing," Brant said through the door. "Do you want me to come in and get yours?"

Why hadn't she thought to put her clothes outside the door before getting into the tub? Now she would either have to get out of the water, wrap herself in a towel and hand her things out to Brant, or let him come in here, where she was taking a bath. By candlelight.

She glanced down at the water. The bubbles completely covered her, except for her head and shoulders. Nothing showed. There was no real reason why he couldn't come in and get the clothes.

"All right, come in," Valerie called, sliding deeper into the water.

BRANT OPENED THE bathroom door. And froze. His gaze slipped immediately to the tub, or rather, to the woman inside.

She looked incredible.

He'd always appreciated Valerie's appearance, always thought she was a beautiful woman, but he'd never seen her looking like this. Never seen her look as womanly as she did at that moment.

She was completely covered. He could see nothing but her head and neck, and here and there, tiny patches of tanned skin where the bubbles had melted. But knowing she was wet and naked beneath those bubbles—and the images that knowledge evoked—was sexier, more arousing than anything he'd ever experienced before.

Candlelight danced in her eyes, mesmerizing him, and for a long moment, Brant stood in the doorway, drinking in the sight of her, the fragrance of her. The essence of her.

She put out a slender arm and pointed toward the floor. "There," she said softly, and for a split second, Brant wondered if she meant for him to kneel beside the tub to worship her beauty.

Then he shook his head slightly, coming to his senses, and realized she meant for him to pick up her wet clothing from the bathroom floor.

He did so in a hurry, knowing that if he lingered any longer, he just might make an even bigger fool of himself.

BY THE TIME VALERIE had gotten out of the bath, the lights had begun to flicker intermittently. Emily had delivered a light supper of ham-and-cheese sandwiches and steaming bowls of vegetable soup to their room, and candles had been lit on the table near the French doors.

Valerie wondered if the touch had been provided because of the failing power, or because of the romantic mood it cast over the room.

Really, this was all too much, she thought, seating herself across the table from Brant. What was it Naomi Gillum had told her? *Your destiny is tied to him.*

Well, destiny was pulling out all the stops. Throwing every cliché in the book at them. Luring them here to this rustic setting, stranding them in a town with only one available room, in an inn run by an incurable romantic. Then taking their clothing, so that they were sitting across from one another with only robes covering their nakedness. Threatening the power, so that candlelight was a necessity. Setting the stage, like something from a Gothic novel.

All that was needed now, Valerie thought acerbically, was a haunting presence to frighten her into Brant's strong, waiting arms.

"You're very quiet tonight," he commented.

Valerie glanced up. The candlelight shifted across his face, making his eyes seem even deeper, more mysterious. Brooding, she thought; in keeping with the atmosphere.

She shivered in spite of herself. "I was just thinking."

"About what happened earlier?"

She nodded. "That man, Remy Devereaux. He tried to kill us, Brant."

If possible, his eyes darkened even more. "I know."

"You realize what that means, don't you? That whoever hired Remy Devereaux—"

"Was willing to kill me to get to you." His voice grew hard. "Yes, I've thought about that, Valerie. I've thought about little else. But I refuse to think my own father would hire someone to kill me."

Valerie could understand his denial. It was difficult to believe your own father could be guilty of murder. She knew that better than anyone. "Your father wasn't the only one involved in the Kingsley investigation," she reminded him. "He isn't the only one who has a vested interest in keeping Cletus Brown behind bars."

"No, you're right," Brant said grimly. "My uncle was also part of the investigation, and though I've never been that close to him, he is still family, and the idea that he might be willing to kill me isn't a particularly comforting one. And as for Hugh Rawlins, he got me into the academy. Did I ever tell you that? He took me under his wing when I first joined the department. He's been more than a mentor to me. He's been a good friend, someone I've always looked up to and admired. If those are my three choices, I have to tell you, Valerie, they all stink."

He got up abruptly from the table and strode to the window, staring out into the darkness. After a moment, Valerie followed him, though, for a while, she didn't say anything. She stared up at his bleak profile, wishing, suddenly, that things could be different between them. Wishing that rebuilding her world didn't include tearing his down.

"Remember that first day I met you," Brant murmured, still staring out at the darkness. "When you were in the hospital and I came to interview you. You said the Kingsley kidnapping had changed a lot of lives. You were right." He turned to face her, his eyes fathomless. "The publicity surrounding the case changed my father. He became obsessed with being a hero, with living up to an image the media created. But nothing in his life ever measured up to that one moment, that one instant when the admiring eyes of an entire country were upon him."

Brant scrubbed his face with his hands, then turned back to the window. "I've sometimes wondered if the reason he was opposed to my becoming a cop wasn't so much that he was afraid I couldn't follow in his footsteps, but because he thought I might somehow overtake them."

Yes, Valerie reflected. She could see how that might happen. She could see how a man like Judd Colter might look into the eyes of his son and see a younger, stronger, better version of himself. And how he might have a hard time accepting it.

A man like Judd Colter might turn against that son, might try to tear down his self-confidence, might be willing to do just about anything to prevent the inevitable comparisons.

But would he be willing to murder his son just to protect his image? His legend?

"Sometimes I've wondered," Brant said slowly, "if the reason I've been so anxious to help you find out the truth is because a secret part of me wants to get back at him. Wants to put a chink in his armor."

"I don't believe that," Valerie said. "You're not that kind of person."

He turned to face her. The look in his eyes sent a chill up Valerie's spine. "A few nights ago you were willing to believe I was capable of murder."

Had it really only been a few nights ago? Had she really once believed him capable of murder?

It seemed impossible now, though Valerie wasn't sure why. Nothing had changed between them, and yet everything had. Somehow, in the last few days, her trust in Brant had begun to grow. She didn't know when or why or how, only that it was so.

And it frightened her. It frightened her badly.

SOMETIME AFTER MIDNIGHT, the haunting presence made its appearance. Though it didn't exactly drive Valerie into Brant's arms, she did wake up with a start and bolt upright in bed at the unexpected noise in the darkness.

The rain had stopped and the moon was out, filling the room with dark, ominous shadows. Valerie could just make out Brant's silhouette at the window.

"What is it?" she asked softly. "What was that noise?"

"Sounded like a motorcycle," he said. "I'm going down to check it out."

He crossed the room to the sofa to draw on the blue robe, and it was only then that Valerie realized he'd been standing at the window naked. She shivered under the covers, pulling the blanket up to her neck as she watched him move toward the door. When he'd disappeared into the hallway, Valerie got out of bed and pulled on her own robe. She followed him into the corridor.

He stood on the landing, staring over the railing into the large living room/lobby below. Valerie joined him. She started to say something, but he motioned her to silence. Together they watched as the front door opened, and a tall, shadowy figure emerged from the darkness.

Valerie could feel Brant tense beside her, and knew he was getting ready to confront the intruder, but just then, another figure appeared from the hallway beneath the stairs. A woman dressed in a white, flowing nightgown.

Valerie recognized Emily, the owner of the inn, and the intruder appeared to be a welcome one. When Emily drew near him, the man took her in his arms and kissed her. Valerie could hear them whispering in the darkness, a low intimate sound that stirred a yearning inside her.

The man swept Emily up into his arms and disappeared with her down the hallway. A door closed softly below, and there was little doubt about the couple's intentions. Little doubt about what they would be doing in a few moments.

The longing grew inside Valerie. She thought she had never felt more lonely than she did just then. She turned to walk back to the room, and Brant followed.

"I would assume," he said dryly, when they'd closed the door behind them, "that was Emily's husband."

"No doubt," Valerie replied, climbing back into bed and pulling the covers over her. She didn't take off her robe, but she saw that Brant did. The fabric slid to the floor with a soft thud, then she heard the springs in the sofa creak ever so slightly as he lay down.

The springs creaked again as he turned over. Then creaked again, as he turned back over. He kicked off the covers, and Valerie heard him curse softly in frustration.

"Do you want me to sleep on the sofa?" she asked.

"No," he said tersely. "That's not what I want."

"This is ridiculous," she said. "I'm smaller than you. The sofa would be more comfortable for me."

"I'll tell you what's ridiculous," Brant said. "It's ridiculous that someone wants to kill you—and now me, it would seem—because of something that happened thirty-one years ago. It's ridiculous to think my father—my *own* father—could be behind it." He sat up on the sofa and stared at her through the darkness. "It's ridiculous that you're over there in that big bed all alone when there's plenty of room for both of us."

Valerie's heart pounded against her chest. "Wh-what?"

"You heard me." Then, "Oh, hell, stop looking at me like that."

"How do you know how I'm looking," she asked, hurt by the angry sting in his words. "You can't even see me."

"No, but I know that look well enough. I saw it the other night in New Orleans. And before that, in the garden at the Kingsley mansion. You're looking as if you think I'll come over there and force my attentions on you."

"Maybe I want you to," Valerie said softly, surprising herself as much as him.

"What?"

"You heard me," she said, using his own words.

"Valerie—"

"Don't say it," she whispered into the darkness. "Don't say anything. Just come over here and kiss me."

It was a request he seemed more than willing to grant. Valerie watched him cross the room toward the bed, felt his weight on the mattress as he climbed under the covers. Then she felt his hand on her arm, and a delicious shiver raced up her spine. He slid his hand down her skin until his fingers found hers, locking them together, drawing her hand up to his mouth to plant soft kisses on each knuckle.

With her free hand, Valerie reached up to cup the back of his neck, pulling him toward her. When his lips were only inches from hers, he released her hand to wrap her tightly in his arms.

And then he kissed her.

And Valerie's whole world shattered.

CHAPTER THIRTEEN

MORNING BROUGHT SUNSHINE. And reality. Valerie awakened with a desperate sense of having done something she shouldn't have. Brant was in bed beside her, sprawled on his back, the covers shoved down to his waist. A sprinkling of dark hair on his chest arrowed its way beneath the covers, and Valerie shivered, remembering the way he'd looked last night. Remembering each and every detail of their lovemaking.

A part of her wanted to wake him up and relive those details, slowly. Over and over again. But another part of her pressed for caution. Yes, they'd made love. Yes, it had been wonderful. Incredible. Earth-moving in every sense of the word.

But nothing could come of it. Nothing could come of a relationship based on dishonesty. She hadn't told Brant the truth about herself, and when she did, he would despise her. He would think she had used him to get to his father.

She got up from the bed and drew on her robe, padding softly across the room to the door to find their clothing in neat stacks outside. Retrieving them, Valerie placed Brant's on the sofa, then took hers into the bathroom and quickly dressed.

He was still asleep when she came back out, and

taking care not to wake him, she opened the French doors and stepped out onto the balcony.

The sky was a pale, rinsed blue, as clear and fragile as crystal. Water droplets shimmered in the trees, refracting the sunlight into a thousand tiny rainbows. The scent of roses wafted from the garden below, and Valerie stood for a long time, drinking in the heady fragrance, and the cool, cleansing mountain air.

After a while, the French doors opened behind her and Brant stepped onto the balcony. Valerie glanced around. He was dressed, too, and judging by the moisture still in his hair, he had just taken a shower.

"How long have you been out here?" He came to stand beside her at the railing, but he didn't touch her. Valerie wasn't sure which emotion was stronger—relief or disappointment.

"For a while," she admitted. "You were sleeping. I didn't want to wake you."

"Why not?"

She shrugged. "I guess I wanted to be alone for a while."

"Having regrets?"

She wished she could look away from his dark gaze, but she couldn't. She shook her head. "Not the kind you mean."

One brow lifted. "Meaning?"

"You told me some things about yourself last night that made me feel closer to you. Made me understand you better. It meant a lot to me that you opened up that way."

"You're not trying to tell me you felt sorry for me, are you? That's not the reason you invited me into your bed, I hope." His tone was teasing, but Valerie sensed there was an edge to his lightness. Almost an urgency.

She shook her head. "No. That's not the reason. That's not the reason at all."

For a moment, heat flooded through Valerie as memories of their lovemaking swept over her. Brant had been so tender with her. So passionate. It had been so easy to lose herself in his kisses, to forget reality in his arms.

His eyes told her that he was remembering, too. And wanting her again.

Valerie drew a trembling breath. "It's just that…I haven't been as open with you. There're things about myself I haven't shared with you, things that maybe I should have told you before we…" Her voice trailed off as she tore her gaze away.

"Made love? You can say it, Valerie. It's nothing to be ashamed of. At least for me, it isn't."

"I'm not ashamed," she said quickly. "Please don't think that."

Gently he cupped her chin with one hand and turned her to face him. "What is it, then?"

At that moment, she wanted to tell him everything, confess who she really was, do her best to make him understand why she had deceived him.

And if it had just been her life on the line, she would have.

So help me, I would, she thought desperately.

But it wasn't just her life. Her father had spent the last thirty-one years—his youth—in prison for a crime he didn't commit. Valerie was his only hope for freedom. If she blew that chance now, she would never forgive herself. She would never be able to live with the knowledge that she'd let her father down.

It was imperative that the Kingsley kidnapping story

be told by Valerie Snow, not by Violet Brown. Who would believe a kidnapper's daughter? Who would believe Cletus Brown's daughter would be unbiased?

The truth about her identity would sabotage any chance she had of making people believe her. Of convincing the public that her father was innocent, and that the three men who had been heralded heroes were responsible for sending him to prison.

One of those men was Brant's father. If she told Brant the truth now, whom would he believe? Her? Or Judd Colter?

BY THE TIME THEY arrived at her duplex in Memphis, the sun was setting. Brant's car was still parked out front, and for the first time, Valerie realized how that must have looked to the neighbors. But she shrugged it off. She didn't know anyone who lived in the neighborhood anyway. What did she care what they thought?

Brant insisted on walking her inside and checking the house before he left. The little red light on the alarm system shone when Valerie opened the door and let them inside. After a thorough check, Brant was satisfied that nothing was amiss.

"I'd better get going," he said, and Valerie walked him to the front door. "I have an early day tomorrow."

"Me, too."

He paused on the threshold, gazing down at her. "About last night...this morning."

"Yes?"

He tunneled his fingers through her hair. "I don't have any regrets, either. Not one."

Valerie closed her eyes as he dipped his head to kiss her goodbye.

NOT FIVE MINUTES AFTER Brant left, Valerie's doorbell rang. Thinking it was Brant, she opened it without checking the peephole. The moment she saw who
stood on the other side, she realized how careless she'd
been.

The blonde standing on the other side looked familiar
to Valerie, but for a moment, she couldn't place her.
Then it came back to her. She was the woman Valerie
had seen with Brant at the fund-raiser, the one who had
come up to him while he'd been dancing with Andrew
Kingsley's wife. The one who had linked her arm possessively through Brant's.

Valerie stared at the blonde now, wondering who she
was, and what on earth she was doing here.

"I'm Kristin Colter," she said. "Austin Colter's wife.
May I come in?"

Valerie tried to suppress her shock. "By all means."
She stepped aside and waved Kristin in.

Kristin's silk dress was misty blue, the exact shade
of her eyes. Pearls shone at her throat and around her
wrist, and her hair was pulled back and fastened with
a pearl comb. She looked regal and elegant and as cold
as ice as she turned in the living room and fixed Valerie
with a frosty stare.

"What do you want?" Valerie asked. She walked into
the living room and stood in front of Kristin, not about
to be intimidated by someone who looked more like a
China doll than a real woman.

"I've been trying to get in touch with you all weekend." Kristin glanced around the duplex. Her gaze came
back to rest on Valerie, reflecting her distaste. "Where
were you?"

"Away," Valerie said evasively.

"With whom?"

Though the question was posed casually enough, Valerie sensed rather than heard the anger behind it. She smiled slightly. "A friend. I still don't understand what you're doing here. Or how it's any of your business who I was with."

If possible, Kristin's gaze grew even colder. A darkness seemed to be simmering just below the surface. "You were with Brant. His car's been parked in front of your house all weekend."

Valerie shrugged. "I guess you have been looking for me, haven't you?"

"Did you sleep with him?"

The bluntness of the question stunned Valerie. She gaped at Kristin for a second before retorting, "I don't see how that's any of your business, either."

"So you did sleep with him," Kristin said, evidently reading more into Valerie's words than she'd intended. Kristin's features hardened with hostility. She held her purse with both hands, and Valerie saw that her knuckles had whitened on the clasp. "He'll never be yours, you know."

"Oh?" Valerie tried to act indifferent, but there was too much going on here—revelations that were very unnerving.

"He's never gotten over me," Kristin said. "He'll never love anyone else. Why do you think he hasn't married in all these years?"

Valerie's heart flip-flopped inside her. So she hadn't imagined the intimacy between them at the fund-raiser. She suddenly felt sick to her stomach. "I didn't realize the two of you had a past."

"We were engaged," Kristin said. "Didn't he tell you? No, I suppose he wouldn't, at that."

"What's the point of this little visit?" Valerie wanted the woman out of her house. She felt dirtied by Kristin's presence. She couldn't stand to think of Brant being with someone like her, holding her in his arms. Making love to Kristin the way he'd made love to her.

Kristin was busy opening her purse. "The point is, how much do you want?"

"I beg your pardon?"

She pulled out a checkbook. "How much do you want to drop this Kingsley-kidnapping nonsense?"

"Let me get this straight," Valerie said slowly. "You're trying to buy me off?"

"That's what you want, isn't it? What other reason could you possibly have for wanting to dredge up all that old business?"

Valerie looked at the woman in disgust. "That 'old business' involved the kidnapping and murder of a child. An innocent man was framed for the crime and sent to prison for life. I'm not after money," she said. "I'm after the truth."

It was as though Kristin hadn't heard a word Valerie said. She pulled the top from a silver pen and opened her checkbook. "I repeat—how much?"

Valerie shoved an angry hand through her hair. The woman's single-mindedness was infuriating. "This isn't about money! It's about justice! Surely you understand the concept. Your husband is a D.A., for God's sake."

That seemed to jolt Kristin from her icy arrogance. She glared at Valerie with open hostility. "My husband is also a Colter. You're trying to destroy his family. I simply won't allow it."

"There may not be anything you can do about it," Valerie replied, folding her arms. Then, realizing she looked too defensive, she dropped them to her sides.

"There's always something I can do." With quick, jerky movements, Kristin shoved the checkbook and pen back into her purse and snapped it closed. "You don't know who you're dealing with."

Valerie thought she had a pretty good idea. A petty, vindictive, spoiled debutante used to getting her own way, primarily because of her looks. A coldly ambitious woman who was only too happy to ride on her husband's coattails, as long as he was on his way to the top.

A woman who might even be willing to resort to violence, to get her own way.

A chill crawled up Valerie's spine, although she was careful to show no outward fear. "You'd better go," she said calmly enough. "Before I call the police."

Kristin laughed, an ugly sound that deepened the chill inside Valerie. "Yes, you do that," she said. "You call the police. Let's see whose side they're on when they get here. I'm a Colter, remember?" She laughed again, but to Valerie's relief, she headed for the door. As she pulled it open, she turned to glance over her shoulder. "I'm warning you. Leave my family alone." Hatred glinted in her eyes as she added, "And stay away from Brant."

AS SOON AS BRANT got to work the next morning, Lieutenant Bermann, his immediate superior in Robbery and Homicide, stuck his head out the door of his glass cubicle and hollered, "Hey, Colter! Captain Rawlins wants to see you ASAP."

Brant got up from his desk and walked down the

hallway to Hugh's office. After knocking on the door, he entered the room, then stopped short just inside. Hugh wasn't alone. Raymond Colter occupied one of the chairs in front of Hugh's desk, and Brant's father sat in the other. Austin Colter stood at the window. He'd been staring down at the street when Brant first entered, but now his gaze locked with Brant's and he scowled in displeasure.

Brant walked slowly across the room to Hugh's desk, and looked down at his father. Although Brant knew his father had been making progress in his physical therapy, he certainly hadn't known that he'd recovered enough to be out and about like this.

Brant thought about the mud and pine needles on the shoes beneath his father's bed the other night, and an uneasiness came over him again. Was it possible his father had been the man in the woods that night? Had he hit Brant over the head to keep from being discovered?

If so, what had he been up to at the Kingsley mansion?

His father's expression gave nothing away. His mouth had been drawn slightly to one side by the stroke, and the lines in his face had deepened, making him look far older than his years. But his eyes were just as dark, just as probing as they'd ever been. He met Brant's gaze now without blinking.

"What's going on?" Brant asked.

His father said nothing, but beside him, Raymond spoke. "That's what we're hoping you'll tell us, Brant."

Brant's gaze shifted to his uncle. Raymond was wearing a dark gray Italian-cut suit with a silk tie and expensive-looking loafers. Brant had never seen his

uncle dress this way before. He looked very successful, very sophisticated; and a comparison to the man
sitting beside him was inevitable. Although there were
only four years separating their ages, Raymond looked
at least twenty years younger than his older brother. And
infinitely stronger.

Brant couldn't help wondering if Raymond had
dressed that way on purpose, if he had intended for the
comparison to be made.

Across the room, Austin Colter, a younger version of
his father, said, "Are you out of your mind? What the
hell are you doing with that Snow woman?"

Brant spared him a glance. "I don't see how that's
any of your damned business."

"No," Hugh said quietly. "But it is my business."

Brant turned back to Hugh. "What's going on here?"
he asked again. "What's this all about?"

Hugh looked down at his desk, as if he couldn't quite
bring himself to meet Brant's eyes. "Are you involved
with Valerie Snow?"

So that was what this was all about, Brant thought,
his anger rising. "Define 'involved.'"

"Dammit, you know what I mean," Hugh said. "This
is serious, Brant."

Brant started to deny it, but then shrugged. "All
right," he conceded. "I might be."

At the window, Austin cursed. Raymond shook his
head sadly, but there was no expression at all on his father's face. He stared straight ahead, unblinking, but his
eyes were bright and alert. He wasn't missing anything,
Brant realized.

"I was afraid of that," Hugh said wearily. "That's

why I'm asking Lieutenant Bermann to take you off her case."

Brant leaned forward suddenly, planting his hands on the surface of Hugh's desk. "You can't do that. Someone's trying to kill her. If you take me off the case, she'll be a sitting duck."

"I'll have Bermann assign someone else to her case," Hugh said. His voice was soft and even, but his expression told Brant he'd made up his mind. There was no use arguing.

But Brant wasn't about to give up without a fight. "That'll take days, maybe even weeks, and you know it. Everyone in the division has a heavy caseload right now. No one's going to be willing to give this case the time and attention it needs."

"Not like you, you mean," said Austin. "Seems to me you were willing to give it plenty of time and attention."

Brant straightened, his hands balling into fists at his sides. He glared down at Hugh. "This is just between you and me, Hugh. What are they doing here?"

"We're worried about you, Brant," said Raymond.

"I'll just bet you are."

"Calm down," Hugh advised softly. "This is for your own good, Brant."

"Is it?" He glared at Hugh, then shifted his focus to first his father, then Raymond and then Austin. "Someone tried to kill us both this weekend." He gauged their expressions carefully. Both Raymond and Austin wore identical masks of shock and Hugh looked worried. Brant glanced at his father, but there was still no reaction.

Hugh said, "All the more reason you should be taken

off this case, Brant. You're too close to it. Too personally involved."

"So I'm just supposed to let Valerie fend for herself to save my own skin, is that it?" he retorted angrily. "Or is there another reason you don't want me on this case? Maybe you think it'll be easier to get to her if I'm not around."

"You're out of line, son," said Raymond.

That last word sent Brant's temper almost to the boiling point. "I am *not* your son," he said through clenched teeth. He glanced at his father and saw him blink once, very slowly, but whether or not there was any significance in the gesture, Brant had no idea.

"Do any of you remember a man named Remy Devereaux?" he asked.

"Devereaux?" Hugh repeated. "You mentioned him the other day. Said you thought you saw him on the street."

"Yeah," Brant said. "Turns out I was right. He tried to run Valerie and me off a mountain road this weekend. He tried to kill us, and I can't help wondering why. Remy was always available for hire, as I recall." He paused, then added, "He's dead, by the way."

Was it Brant's imagination or had his uncle breathed a sigh of relief? Had Hugh looked quickly away to avoid Brant's eyes? Had the smirk on his cousin's face deepened?

And what about his father? What was his reaction to the news of Remy Devereaux?

"What are you getting at?" Austin demanded.

"I think that's pretty clear," Brant said. "Valerie Snow is trying to uncover the truth about what happened the night Adam Kingsley was kidnapped. Remy Devereaux was hired to stop her."

"Are you saying you think one of us had something to do with it?" Raymond asked in disbelief.

Brant shrugged. "I don't want to think that. And I wouldn't have, if not for this little ambush today. You're all acting guilty as hell." He strode across the room, leaving dead silence in his wake. When he reached the door, he glanced back as Hugh called his name.

"No matter what you think about us, you're off the case, Brant. That's the end of it."

"Is it?" Brant opened the door. "You seem to be forgetting that when I'm off duty, my time is my own."

"I don't have to tell you what could happen if you interfere in someone else's case," Hugh warned. "We're talking possible suspension."

"We both know that's not going to happen," Brant replied. "Because Valerie's case isn't going to be assigned to anyone else, is it?"

He strode out the door and was halfway down the hall when someone grabbed his arm from behind. Brant whirled, shaking off the hand. "Get your hand off me," he said to his cousin.

Austin sneered. "Don't think I don't know what all this is about. Why you're so anxious to side with the enemy and make the rest of us look bad."

"I don't know what the hell you're talking about," Brand said. "Nor do I care."

"This is about Kristin, isn't it?"

Brant just shook his head. "You don't know how far off the mark you are, Austin."

Austin's eyes darkened with anger. "She told me, you know. She told me all about how you came sniffing around when we were separated, begging her to take you back, trying to force yourself on her. It must have killed you when we got back together. It must have killed you that she chose me over you—not once, but twice."

"Your ego is only exceeded by your stupidity," Brant said. "I've had enough of this." He turned to go, but Austin grabbed him again.

Brant glanced down at Austin's hand on his arm. Then slowly he lifted his gaze. "I'll only say this once more. Get your hand off me."

Something in his face must have alarmed Austin, for he did as he was told. But he didn't back away. He glared at Brant defiantly. "You're trying to ruin me," he accused. "You've always resented me because of Kristin. And because you know I'm the son *your* father always wanted. That's it, isn't it? You're siding with that woman to get back at me. To sabotage my campaign. Why don't you just tell the press you think our fathers are guilty? But then, you don't have to, do you? Your actions speak louder than words."

"As usual, you're wrong on so many counts, I wouldn't know where to start to straighten you out," Brant said coldly.

"I'm on to you," Austin said. "This is all working out perfectly for you, isn't it? You get to ruin my career and discredit your father all at the same time. And the fact that you're taking down my father and Hugh Rawlins is just a minor detail, isn't it? Hell, you're even getting to sleep with the woman who's out to destroy us all—"

Brant slammed Austin up against the wall, his hands grabbing the lapels of Austin's expensive suit. "I advise you to shut your mouth," he said almost calmly, "before I shut it for you."

"Let him go," ordered a slurred voice from down the hallway.

Brant turned to see his father walking toward them. His steps were slow and measured, but he was managing without a walker or a cane. For a moment, seeing his father looking almost like his old self threw Brant. He stared at him in shock.

"Let him go," his father said again as he neared them. Even though his words were slurred, his voice was strong and deep, much as it had always been.

Brant turned to Austin. He released his suit coat and stepped back, gazing at his cousin in disgust.

Judd glared at both of them. "Look at the two of you. Acting like kids."

"Tell him to stay away from my wife," Austin said angrily.

Brant started to retort, but Judd pointed his finger at them. "Shut up," he said. "Shut up, the both of you." His gaze shifted to Austin. "Get out of here, Austin."

"But—"

Judd Colter, even recovering from a stroke, was still a powerful presence. He said nothing, just glared at Austin, and with a sullen expression, Austin turned and disappeared down the hallway.

Brant turned back to his father. "It's not true. What he said about Kristin—"

His father cut him off with a snort. "Never thought it was. A she-devil like that would cause a man nothing but misery. You're better off without her."

"I figured that out about two minutes after she broke our engagement," Brant said. "But everyone in the family seems to think I've carried a torch for her all these years."

"Fools," Judd snapped. "The lot of them."

Brant looked at him in surprise. He never thought he would see the day when his father would take his side over the rest of the family. "You've made a lot of progress," he said. "I had no idea you could get around like this."

"My physical therapist says I'm too ornery to keep down for long," Judd replied.

Brant grimaced. He could believe that. "Do you need a ride home?"

"Raymond'll take me when I'm ready to go. He's been very…helpful these days."

Something in his tone caused Brant to glance at him sharply. Had his father noticed his brother's solicitude toward Brant's mother?

"Let's walk outside," he said to Brant. "I want to talk to you."

They started down the hall to the elevators, Brant taking care to keep his own steps slow, matching his father's. Several officers stopped them on the way out to remark on Judd's recovery, and it was several minutes before they were able to leave the building. Judd pointed to a bench across the street. "I'm tuckered out," he said. "Let's sit."

They crossed the street and sat down on the bench. The July day was hot and humid, and it seemed even more so after having left an air-conditioned building. A light breeze drifted over the pavement, stirring the hot air and carrying the scent of the river.

Brant said, "What did you want to talk to me about?"

"What happened back there. It must have seemed like we were all ganging up on you." The slur in his words was more pronounced now, and Brant wondered if it was because his father was tired. Or had he been taking pains to hide it earlier because of his pride?

Brant thought about Valerie's accusation—that his father and his uncle and Hugh Rawlins had sent an innocent man to prison because their pride wouldn't allow them to admit they'd made a mistake.

"Hugh took you off the case because he didn't want this thing hurting your career."

Brant glanced at him. "A woman could get killed. I'm not much worried about my career right now."

"Maybe she's not in danger anymore. You said Remy Devereaux is dead."

"Yes," Brant said quietly. "But whoever hired him is still alive."

His father turned to him. His eyes were clouded with what Brant could only assume was worry. "You're not going to give up on this, are you?"

Brant shrugged. "Would you?"

His father didn't answer. Instead he watched the traffic on the street and said, "Being a cop, especially a good one, is a hard way of life, Brant. I expect you've learned that by now. It's not only what you do, but who you are. People on the outside, they don't understand. Your mother never did."

Was that wistfulness in his father's voice? Regret? Brant was hard-pressed to believe it, but how else to explain the quiver? The stroke? Fatigue?

Brant said, "Maybe if you'd talked to her the way you just did with me, she would have. Maybe she still would."

His father shrugged. "I'm an old man, Brant. A tired, sick, old man. I don't have much to offer anymore. Hell,

I don't have anything to offer. Your mother's a fine woman, but it's too late for explanations."

"It's never too late."

His father turned to him, and their eyes met in understanding. *He knows,* Brant thought. *He knows what Raymond is up to.*

Brant said almost fiercely, "She's still your wife."

His father said nothing. He returned his gaze to the street. After a moment, Brant asked, "Why are you telling me all this? Why now?"

Judd drew a long, weary breath. "You're a good cop, Brant. A damned good cop. I expect I don't have much more time."

"What are you talking about? Your recovery's been nothing short of miraculous. The doctors said it might take years—" He stopped short when he saw his father's expression. Somehow Brant knew he wasn't talking about his health.

"I expect I don't have much more time."

Before the truth comes out, Brant silently added.

Their gazes met for one last time. Tears shimmered in his father's eyes, and as Brant watched, one spilled over and ran down the old man's weathered face.

CHAPTER FOURTEEN

THE DAY HAD SLIPPED away before Valerie was able to reach Brant on his cell phone.

"Where've you been?" she asked impatiently. "I've been trying to reach you for hours."

"I do have other cases," he snapped.

"Sorry," Valerie murmured, stung by his retort.

She heard him sigh. "No, I'm sorry. It's been a bad day. I'll tell you about it when I see you. Where are you?"

"I'm at the main library," she said, excitement creeping into her voice. "How soon can you get over here? I've found something."

"I'm on my way."

VALERIE SAT BEHIND a monitor at the library, and Brant leaned over her. "What have you found?" he asked.

A delicious shiver coursed through her at his nearness. His warm breath fanned the back of her neck, and Valerie knew if she turned her head ever so slightly, she could touch her lips to his.

The desire to do so was almost overwhelming. But she could tell something was wrong. Brant didn't seem himself. His eyes were distant, his expression carefully blank.

She shifted in her chair, putting some distance

between them so that she could turn and look up at him without temptation. "What's wrong?"

He hesitated. "I've been taken off your case."

Valerie stared at him in disbelief. "After what happened this weekend? Why?"

"My superiors seem to think I'm too personally involved. With you," he added, his gaze meeting hers.

Valerie swallowed, her heart beating in her throat. "What did you tell them?"

"I told them I might be." He lowered his head suddenly and kissed her, almost savagely, as if to convince himself whether he was or not.

He might still have doubts, Valerie thought dazedly. But she certainly didn't.

She'd fallen for Brant Colter in a big way, and he still had no earthly idea who she was.

The thought jarred her and she pulled back, glancing around to see if anyone had seen them. Her gaze returned to Brant. There was something in his eyes that made her uneasy. She said worriedly, "Something else happened, didn't it? You seem upset."

He straightened. "You don't think getting removed from a case is reason enough to be upset?"

"Yes, of course, it is," Valerie said. "But I get the feeling there's more to it than that."

Brant shrugged. "It's no big deal. Show me what you've found."

So that was that, Valerie thought, feeling oddly disappointed. Almost betrayed. He'd opened up to her to a certain point, but not beyond.

Well, what did you expect? she asked herself angrily. *You haven't exactly been forthcoming with him, now have you?*

She forced her attention back to the monitor, where she'd been scrolling through newspaper articles from thirty-one years ago. Backing up the pages, she located the one she wanted.

"Look." She nodded toward the screen. Although her excitement was dampened by Brant's mood, she still felt a little quiver of nerves as she stared at the article and accompanying picture.

Valerie had already read the article so many times, she practically knew it by heart. She watched Brant's expression as he scanned the lines about a little boy named Johnny Wayne Tyler who had been missing for two days. The date of the article was one week to the day after Adam Kingsley had been kidnapped.

When Brant finished reading, he looked up. "I see what you're getting at," he said. "The timing would have been about right. But it says here, this boy was five years old. Two years older than Adam Kingsley."

"Yes, but look at his picture. You can tell he's small for his age. And remember what James Denver said about the autopsy. It was rushed, and since the body had already been identified, the M.E. would have only been concentrating on cause of death. Besides, forensic science wasn't nearly as sophisticated back then as it is now. He could have just missed it. Or maybe he didn't," Valerie said. "Maybe he noted something in his report that was a cause of concern. Maybe that's why the autopsy report and pictures of the body are missing from the police file."

"It says here that the boy's stepfather was the prime suspect in the disappearance. Child Welfare had been alerted to possible abuse in the home on two previous occasions. The boy had sustained injuries before, serious enough to require medical treatment."

Valerie nodded. "Yeah, I checked. No arrest was ever made because the boy's body was never found."

Brant straightened and ran a tired hand through his hair. "So what do we have here? If Johnny Wayne Tyler was buried in Adam Kingsley's grave, that means someone who had access to Adam—or to his body—removed his personal effects and put them on Johnny. That's more than just a cover-up," he said grimly. "We're talking about the kidnapping itself."

Valerie had never seen his eyes look so haunted. She knew exactly what he was thinking. It was bad enough to consider the possibility that his father had been part of a conspiracy to send an innocent man to prison. But it was sheer agony to think that he could have been in on the kidnapping. The murder of little Adam Kingsley.

Probably no one in the world could understand what he was feeling at that moment better than Valerie.

She stood and put a hand on his arm, felt him stiffen beneath her touch. He didn't pull away, but the message was loud and clear.

Tears stung Valerie's eyes at his rejection. Dear God, she thought miserably. How had things gotten so complicated? They were getting so close to the truth, but the closer they got, the further away they would drift. And when Brant found out the truth about her—

He stared down at her, his eyes still distant, his expression resolved. "Where do we go from here?"

"I want to exhume the body," Valerie said.

"You heard what Denver said. An exhumation won't be easy. We'll have to contact the Kingsleys—"

"I've already done that. Neither Edward nor Iris

would talk to me, but their attorney has agreed to see me this evening in his office. Will you come with me?" she asked hesitantly, not certain what to expect from him now.

His gaze never wavered from hers. "You couldn't keep me away."

THE KINGSLEY FAMILY attorney, Victor Northrup, was a tall, trim, taciturn man of about sixty. His silver hair and mustache contrasted dramatically with his deeply tanned skin and eyes so light a gray they almost appeared colorless. His direct, unwavering gaze was very unnerving.

Brant and Valerie sat across from his enormous desk as he studied them over the tips of his steepled fingers. Another man was also present, and Northrup introduced him as Jeremy Willows, an associate with the law firm of Northrup, Simmons and Fitzgerald. But Brant recognized him as Edward Kingsley's stepson.

He didn't join them at Northrup's desk, but remained standing across the room, one arm resting on the marble mantel of a fireplace. He, like Northrup, was dressed in a dark suit, white, starched shirt and conservative striped tie—the standard uniform of the upscale lawyer, although instead of wing tips, Brant noticed that Willows wore tasseled loafers.

Brant turned his attention back to Northrup, who was addressing Valerie in a manner that was icily condescending.

"That you would even suggest such a thing to my clients is inconceivable."

Valerie sat forward, her expression earnest, but Brant saw her knuckles whiten where she clasped her purse in her lap. "Did you read the information I faxed over to you? Did the Kingsleys even see it? Mr. Northrup, we've every reason to believe the body buried in that grave is not Adam Kingsley's. Surely your clients would want to know this."

If possible, his voice grew even colder. "Adam Kingsley is dead, Ms. Snow. He has been for thirty-one years. His rest will not be disturbed so that you and your shoddy newspaper can have a new headline. Now, if you'll excuse me, I don't think there's anything further to discuss."

Valerie stood to leave, but Brant wasn't quite finished. "We can get a court order if we have to," he said. "We don't have to obtain your client's permission to exhume that body. We came here as a courtesy."

Northrup smiled. "There isn't a court in this state that would grant you such permission, and if I were you, I would be careful with my threats, Sergeant Colter. You and I both know my client could have your badge with one phone call."

"That may be," Brant said. "But you can tell 'your client,' this isn't over. The truth will come out, one way or another."

"HE'S RIGHT, YOU KNOW," Valerie said gloomily, as she and Brant stood beside his car in the parking garage. "We'll never get a court order to exhume that body."

"Not without more proof," Brant agreed. "But it's not like you to give up."

"I'm not giving up," Valerie said. "But even if we did exhume the body and even if we found out it isn't Adam Kingsley's, that still doesn't prove Cletus Brown's innocence."

"No," Brant agreed. "But it might be reason enough to petition for a retrial. He was convicted of Adam Kingsley's murder. Without a body, murder is pretty hard to prove."

Valerie glanced up at him. "You sound as though you're beginning to believe Cletus Brown is innocent."

Brant shrugged. "I don't know what I believe. But there are things about his conviction that bother me. At the very least, I think he deserves a new trial."

The admission was so astonishing, Valerie didn't know what to say at first. And then it came to her what she had to say. What is was past time to say.

"You don't know how much it means to me to hear you say that," she said softly. "There's something I have to tell you. Something I should have told you before, but—"

The sound of a car engine drowned out her words. Valerie stopped and glanced around as a bright red sports car came tearing through the parking garage and halted right beside them. The door opened, and Andrew Kingsley emerged.

"I thought I might find you here," he said as he walked toward them.

Valerie made the introduction. The two men shook hands. "You're acquainted with my wife, I believe," Andrew said to Brant.

Brant nodded. "Hope and I go way back."

Andrew looked as if he wanted to comment, but changed his mind. He turned to Valerie instead and handed her a manila envelope. "I believe this is what you need."

Valerie stared down at the envelope, then raised her gaze to Andrew's. "What is it?"

"A signed affidavit from my father, giving you permission to exhume Adam's body."

Valerie's mouth dropped in shock. For a moment she gaped at him, then said, "How did you manage it?"

Andrew shrugged. "Don't ask. Suffice it to say, I have some information—never mind what kind—that I find useful once in a while in getting my old man to do things he wouldn't ordinarily be inclined to do. There are two conditions, however, that I must insist upon."

"Such as?" Brant asked suspiciously.

"First, that a forensic expert of my choosing be allowed to conduct the autopsy. I've already contacted Dr. Henry Wu from Boston, and he's agreed to fly down here tonight. Arrangements have been made with Mercy General Hospital to use their facilities as soon as Dr. Wu arrives. I've also arranged for him to have Adam's medical records. Any objections so far?"

Valerie glanced at Brant. He shook his head. "I've heard of Dr. Wu's work. His credentials are impeccable."

"The second condition?" Valerie asked.

"That whatever the findings, nothing will be made public until you contact me."

Valerie nodded. "Agreed."

"Then I guess that's that."

He turned to leave, but Brant asked, "Why are you doing this?"

Andrew drew a long breath. "I think Ms. Snow can answer that question as well as I."

Valerie smiled in understanding. "I don't know how I can thank you for this."

"Find out what happened to Adam," he said. "That's all the thanks I need."

EDWARD KINGSLEY'S signature cut through an amazing amount of red tape. Valerie was astonished by how quickly everything was arranged. It was agreed that the body would be exhumed at night, with as few witnessess as was legally possible to prevent the story from being leaked to the press.

Within a matter of hours, the body had been transported to Mercy General Hospital where Dr. Henry Wu awaited to commence the autopsy.

Valerie and Brant waited in a small room outside the morgue. Brant paced nervously while Valerie sat and watched him. She thought about earlier, when she had tried to tell him who she was, but then Andrew Kingsley had arrived, and since then, things had been happening too quickly.

And somehow, now just didn't seem the right time. The body of a child lay beyond those double doors, and whether it was Adam Kingsley's or Johnny Wayne Tyler's, the fact remained that a child had been murdered thirty-one years ago. Valerie couldn't help thinking about what each of those poor little boys had gone through, the terror they had experienced before their tiny lives had been extinguished.

She glanced up as Dr. Wu came through the double doors. Valerie stood and walked over to him. "It's over?"

Dr. Wu shook his head. "No, but I do have some preliminary findings you might be interested in."

Brant came up behind Valerie. "What is it?"

"First of all, the child in question wasn't three years old at the time of death. I'd put his age closer to five. Second of all, he had several bone fractures that had healed before time of death, including a broken leg and a broken arm. It's my guess he didn't receive proper medical treatment. The bone in his leg knitted badly. The child walked with a limp."

"You're sure about this?" Brant asked.

Dr. Wu nodded. "Absolutely."

"How could the medical examiner have missed something like that in the first autopsy?" Valerie asked.

"We've come a long way in thirty-one years in determining age," Dr. Wu said. "But even back then, the bone fractures would have been detected. Unless, of course, a full autopsy wasn't performed."

"That's possible," Brant said. "We were told the autopsy was rushed, that the M.E. was looking primarily for cause of death. An identification had already been made."

Dr. Wu glanced at Brant. "An incorrect identification, it would seem. I've looked at Adam Kingsley's medical records. He had no broken bones, no serious injuries of any kind. There is no way that body can be his. Absolutely no way."

THE KINGSLEYS WERE stunned by the revelation. Andrew had insisted that the entire family be present to hear what Valerie and Brant had learned. He already knew, of course. As per their agreement, Valerie had called and informed him of their findings. He'd then asked her and Brant to drive out to the mansion to be present when he broke it to the family, in case there were questions.

Jeremy Willows took it calmly enough. He stood apart from the gathering, much as he had in Victor Northrup's office yesterday. But Valerie knew that he was watching them, taking in every word that was said.

Pamela Kingsley, Jeremy's mother, burst into tears. "I was the one who found him missing, you know. That night has *haunted* me. I've asked myself a thousand times if I'd gone up earlier, would I have been able to save him?" She broke down again, and Edward, who had aged ten years on hearing the news, absently patted her hand. His face was completely ashen, and Valerie worried that he might be on the verge of a heart attack.

But it was Iris Kingsley, Adam's grandmother, who concerned her the most. After one strangled cry, the old woman fell completely silent, her arms wrapped around her middle, her frail body swaying to and fro, as if she were rocking an invisible child in her arms.

Valerie thought her heart would break at the sight. She turned away, tears stinging her eyes.

As gently as he could, Brant related the events that had led to the autopsy and what Dr. Wu had learned. When there were no more questions, Andrew showed them out.

Valerie said softly, "Is she going to be okay?"

"Grandmother?" Andrew's smile was more of a grimace. "She's a survivor. She'll get through this. We all will. In time." He turned to Brant. "What happens now?"

"Both cases will have to be reopened. We think the body in Adam's grave is that of a boy named Johnny Wayne Tyler, who disappeared around the same time

Adam did. We've contacted Johnny's family, and his mother has agreed to cooperate. Dr. Wu will do the DNA testing."

"This is going to be a nightmare for my family," Andrew said. He glanced at Brant. "What do you think the chances are that Adam could still be alive after all these years?"

Brant hesitated. "Not very good, I'm afraid."

"There is a chance, though."

"A very slim one."

"That's more than we've had for the last thirty-one years," Andrew said quietly.

CHAPTER FIFTEEN

VALERIE HADN'T BEEN home in almost thirty-six hours.
She hadn't had any sleep, either, and as she let herself
in the front door, she felt punch-drunk. Too exhausted
to remain on her feet, but too keyed up to rest.

She typed in the code on the alarm and watched as
the red light turned to green, then entered another code
that would arm the doors and windows, but wouldn't
activate the motion detector.

She thought about what Brant had said yesterday,
or had it been this morning? That if the body in the
grave didn't belong to Adam Kingsley, at the very least
a retrial could be declared for her father.

Of course, Brant hadn't known they were talking
about her father. Valerie still hadn't told him who she
was, but there was really no point in holding back now.
She knew she could trust him with the truth. He'd proven
himself over and over.

First thing in the morning, Valerie would take everything she'd discovered—including her mother's diary—
to her father's attorney, so that he could begin what
would likely be a long legal process. Then she would go
see Brant, tell him everything, and hope for the best.

Somehow she would find a way to make him understand. She had to. Because they'd been through too much

to let things end badly. She couldn't bear the thought of Brant hating her, despising her.

She couldn't bear to think of him not being in her life; but that could very well be the consequence of her deception.

Then don't, she told herself firmly. *Don't think about it.*

What good did it do to dwell on the worst-case scenario? Wasn't it better to hope for the best?

Valerie took a deep breath and headed for the shower, where she stood in the steaming water so long her fingers began to shrivel. Toweling off, she pulled on her bathrobe and went out to the kitchen to fix herself a cup of tea. She carried the cup with her into the bedroom, got out the box of her mother's personal effects she'd hidden in her closet, and tried to decide if there was anything among the myriad of books, articles and mementos, other than her mother's diary, that she needed to give to her father's attorney.

Valerie pulled the box to the middle of the floor and sat down, cross-legged, to go through once more the newspaper clippings and documents her mother had collected over the years. The diary was still in the kitchen, safely in the canister where she'd returned it when she'd gotten back from New Orleans. When she'd first arrived in Memphis, she'd thought it was better not to keep her mother's journal with the rest of the things, in case someone managed to break into her house. They might find the box of articles and mementos, but she didn't think they would ever find the diary.

Along with the newspaper clippings and books about the kidnapping, there were also some personal effects of her father's, including his wallet. For a long time after

Valerie had read her mother's diary, she hadn't been able to go through his things, to open that wallet and see what remained of the life her father had led before he'd been sent to prison.

Finally, though, after moving to Memphis, she'd gotten up her courage and had opened the wallet one night. There were two one-dollar bills inside, along with his driver's license, his social security card and a picture of Valerie and her mother.

That photo had almost been Valerie's undoing. Everything that had been taken from her had come rushing back to her, and she'd closed the wallet, putting it away until another time when she felt stronger, more able to cope with her rage at Judd Colter for what he had done to her family.

Valerie opened the wallet now, fingering the cheap imitation leather, flipping through the windows that contained the picture of her and her mother, the driver's license and the social security card. She checked the money holder. The two dollars were still inside. Everything was exactly as it had been the night her father had been arrested.

Two measly dollars in his wallet, Valerie thought. Where had the fifteen thousand dollars in the trunk of his car come from? Who had planted it there?

She started to put the wallet away, but something metal fell out of one of the compartments. A coin. Valerie frowned. She'd checked the wallet before. There had been nothing else inside. No money except for the two one-dollar bills.

But then, she hadn't examined the wallet as closely as she might have. She could have missed some change tucked away in one of the compartments.

Picking up the coin from the floor, Valerie started to stuff it back into the wallet, then froze. This was no ordinary coin. It had a face on one side, but the other side was blank, and a tiny hole had been drilled through the top, so that a chain could slip through.

A one-sided coin.

I've always thought that if I could just find it, I'd know once and for all what really happened to Adam.

The horror rose up inside her so quickly, Valerie almost didn't make it to the bathroom before she was violently ill. Afterward, her legs trembled so badly she could scarcely stand, her hands shook so she could hardly wet a cloth and press it to her face.

She stared at her pale reflection in the mirror for a long time as a voice inside her head mocked her.

"Tainted!" it screamed. "You have the tainted blood of a killer in your veins!"

HOW COULD SHE HAVE BEEN so wrong? Valerie wondered hours later as she lay in bed, unable to sleep. She put her hands to her face and squeezed her eyes tightly shut, trying to blot out what she'd discovered.

"Dear God, what have I done?" she whispered into the darkness. She'd set about to destroy three men's reputations, and for what? Some misguided notion of loyalty and justice. Her father was a killer. She'd held the proof in her own hand, and no amount of scrubbing had been able to remove the imprint of that medallion from her skin.

She rubbed her hands across her face, staring into the darkness. She had proof of her father's guilt, but the question was, what was she going to do with it? He was already in prison, serving a life sentence without parole. Would coming forward with the coin make any difference? Would justice be better served?

Dear God, what was she thinking? Of course, she had to come forward. The autopsy had proven the body in Adam's grave wasn't his, so that meant her father would, in all likelihood, be given a new trial. He might even be cleared because of the inconsistencies in the case, such as the missing autopsy report and pictures from the police file. Could she really be a party to that? Could she let a murderer—even her own father—go free?

She was doing exactly what she'd been worried Brant would do. Concealing evidence. If given proof of his father's guilt, what would he have done with it?

That was no longer a question. Valerie knew beyond a shadow of a doubt that Brant would have had the courage to do the right thing. He would have chosen justice over pride and loyalty. Could Valerie really do any differently?

But was she as courageous as Brant? Could she face the questions, the accusations, the cruel taunts that she and her mother had once run away from?

Could she face the disgust in Brant's eyes when he learned the truth?

VALERIE AWAKENED sometime later to find a shadow standing over her. She'd been dreaming about Adam Kingsley, as a grown man. He looked just like Andrew, but she knew he was Adam because he was pointing an accusing finger at her.

"Your father killed me!" he shouted. "What are you going to do about it?"

The dream seemed so real that when Valerie awakened, she thought it was Adam Kingsley's ghost standing over her. Then the shadow moved into a patch of moonlight, and her terror deepened. She tried to scream, but he was on her before she could utter a sound. His eyes, as cold and dark as the Mississippi River on a moonless night, glared down at her.

"Don't make a sound," he warned, pointing a gun at her. "Understand?"

She saw the cruelty in those dark eyes and didn't dare provoke him. She nodded slowly.

Just as slowly, Austin Colter took his gloved hand from her mouth.

"How did you get in here?" Valerie gasped, clutching the sheet to her throat.

"My father owns the company that installed your security system. It was a simple matter of getting into the computer and finding out the code. I've been in here before, by the way. Several times."

Valerie stared at him in horror. "Why?"

He shrugged and looked around. "I see you found the little gift I left for you." Moonlight glinted on the gold medallion he held up.

Fear clawed at her spine. "How did you know about the coin?"

"I put it there," he said matter-of-factly. "After your first article came out, I came in here looking for something to use against you, and surprise, surprise. I discovered you're none other than Cletus Brown's daughter. Only I wasn't quite prepared to use that little tidbit. I was afraid it might backfire on me, and besides, I didn't think that would stop your investigation. But I figured if you became convinced your father really did murder Adam Kingsley, you'd have to give it up. What was it Andrew told you in the nursery the night of my fund-raiser? 'Find the coin and you find my brother's killer?'"

"Something like that," Valerie whispered. Dear God, what was he saying? That her father was innocent? The coin had been planted in his wallet to make her think he was guilty? That was exactly what she'd thought. She'd almost gone to the police tonight with the evidence, but something had stopped her. Something had warned her to wait until morning.

Valerie closed her eyes as a wave of emotion rolled over her.

Austin sat down on the edge of her bed, almost as if he were an old friend settling in for a chat. "It might interest you to know that I found the coin years ago, only I never knew its significance until I overheard you and Andrew talking that night."

"I don't understand," she said, her heart beating like the wings of a caged bird inside her chest.

"It's very simple, Valerie. I found that medallion in my father's safe years ago. Now, do you understand?"

Valerie looked at him with dawning horror. "Your father—"

"Kidnapped and murdered Adam Kingsley." Austin shrugged. "It all fits, when you think about it. He'd worked for the Kingsleys for years as a security guard when he was off duty. He knew the layout of the house, all about the fund-raiser that night, everything. And then he was assigned to the case, along with his brother and one of his best friends. How perfect could that be? He knew exactly how to lead their investigation in the wrong direction, how to create confusion at the ransom drop, so that Edward Kingsley was isolated from the police just long enough for my father to take the money.

The police never could figure out how the kidnapper got inside the net without their seeing him, or how he escaped. But he was already inside the net. He was one of them."

Valerie's head whirled in confusion. If Raymond Colter was the murderer, why was Austin Colter holding a gun on her?

"Then he found himself a patsy," Austin was saying. "He planted part of the ransom money in Brown's car and made an anonymous phone call to his brother. My uncle was always so full of himself, he never stopped to consider how he was being yanked around like a puppet. He thought he was solving the second crime of the century. My God, the man's ego was incredible after that. I don't see how my father kept from telling him the truth, just to watch him deflate."

"I guess your father used the ransom money to start his own security business," Valerie said.

Austin nodded. "I would assume so."

"He hired Remy Devereaux to kill me."

"Actually, no. He hired Remy to frighten you into leaving town. I knew about it. We all did—Kristin, Hugh Rawlins and me. Dad told us about it the night of my fund-raiser, in Kinglsey's study. Oh, not about the kidnapping, of course, but that he'd hired Remy to run you out of town because he was worried what the publicity would do to my campaign and to Uncle Judd's health. Remy was demanding more money, and Dad was worried that he'd gotten in over his head. He wanted Hugh to strong-arm Remy and run him out of town again. But I decided to cut my own deal with Remy. On the QT, of course."

"And your deal was for him to kill me," she said. "And Naomi Gillum."

"Remy followed you to New Orleans. When he found out about Naomi, he knew she'd have to go."

Brant had been right, Valerie thought. Remy had been inside the apartment when she and Naomi had talked. And then later, after he'd killed her, Valerie had seen him leaving.

She shuddered, feeling ill. "What about Brant? Did you hire Remy to kill him as well?"

Austin smiled. "That would have been a bonus."

"Why?" Valerie asked desperately. "You had nothing to do with the kidnapping. Why would you want me dead? I wasn't a threat to you."

She saw his face contort in rage. "Of course, you were. Do you think the Party would look at me twice if there was even a hint of scandal attached to my name? If you'd uncovered the truth about my father, my career would have been dead on arrival. Much like you're going to be, I'm afraid."

He stood and loomed over her, placing the gun against her temple. "Get up."

There was no mistaking the warning in his voice. Valerie, searching her mind frantically for a means of escape, did as she was told. But when she was on her feet, he looped an arm around her throat and kept the gun at her temple. "We're going into the living room," he said. "Nice and slow."

Valerie started toward the bedroom door. The living room beyond was illuminated with a soft, bluish light. She hadn't used her computer in days, so obviously Austin had turned it on.

"It's waiting for you," he said. He guided her toward

the computer. When they got to her desk, he increased the pressure against her throat. "Sit down."

Valerie sat and stared at the screen. Fear jumbled the words before her eyes and it took her a moment to focus. But her terror turned to horror as she read what Austin Colter had written. It was a suicide note. Hers.

It stated that she couldn't go on because she'd found proof her father really had murdered Adam Kingsley. She was afraid that she was like him, that she had inherited a murderer's genes, and that eventually she, too, might kill.

"My God," she whispered, thinking how closely the words matched the way she'd felt for thirty-one years. How had he known? she thought. How had Austin discovered her deepest, darkest fear?

Valerie felt the cold metal of the gun against her temple, and she squeezed her eyes shut. He was going to kill her. In a moment she would be dead.

But not without a fight, she decided. She wouldn't make it easy for him. She would not die and let Brant believe her a coward.

Her eyes fell on the letter opener on her desk, and she readied herself to spring for it. Then suddenly, she felt a draft of air on the back of her neck, heard a telltale creak as the front door slowly opened.

Austin heard it, too. She sensed more than felt his hand on the gun tense, and her heart nearly stopped.

"Drop it," Brant said.

Slowly, Austin turned to face Brant, but he kept his arm around Valerie's throat. "This doesn't concern you," he said.

"Like hell it doesn't." Brant moved around the room, keeping his gun pointed at Austin.

"I'll shoot her," Austin warned.

"No, you won't. It's all over."

"Not if I kill you both." Valerie felt his arm tighten around her neck.

"Two deaths won't be so easy to explain," Brant said. "Let her go."

"Do you know who she is?" Austin asked. "Do you know what the woman you're trying to protect has done to you?"

Valerie closed her eyes. *No,* she thought. *Please, no. Not like this.*

"Her name is Violet Brown. Isn't that right?" Austin's arm tightened against her throat even more. "Isn't it?"

Valerie closed her eyes as pain ripped through her. *"Isn't it?"*

She could only manage a weak nod. His arm was cutting off her wind, and she knew in a moment she would pass out.

But then, incredibly, Austin's grip eased. "She's Cletus Brown's daughter, Brant. Don't you see? She's been playing you for a fool all along, using you to destroy your own father. She's lied to you from the beginning."

Valerie could feel Brant's eyes on her. She forced her gaze to meet his.

"Is that true?" he asked.

"Answer him," Austin commanded, the muscles in his arm tensing.

Valerie nodded. "It's true," she said painfully. "My real name is Violet Brown."

In the soft glow of the computer screen, she saw something in Brant's dark eyes she couldn't bear. Hate. Disgust. Betrayal. Then his gaze returned to Austin.

"That doesn't justify what you were about to do. Let her go," he said again.

"She'll ruin us all," Austin replied. She could hear the desperation and fear in his voice, and knew that he could easily be pushed into doing something stupid.

Brant knew it, too. He lowered his gun to his side. "Let's both put down the guns. Let's talk about this for a moment. There's got to be some other way."

Valerie felt Austin hesitate. "What other way?"

"We're Colters," Brant said. "I'm a cop and you're a D.A. We can figure this thing out. Discredit her somehow. Use who she is against her. Look at the resources we have between us. By the time we get finished with her, it won't matter what she writes. No one will believe a word she says. Hell, we can probably even get her thrown in jail, right alongside her old man."

Valerie wanted to believe that Brant was just trying to buy them both some time; that he was, in actuality, trying to save her life. But the cold, empty look he gave her made her shudder with dread. Made her wonder if she'd pushed him too far.

"I don't believe you," Austin said. "You've never been that kind of cop."

"I've never been made a fool of by a woman out to destroy my family," Brant returned. "I don't much care for the feeling."

Again Austin hesitated, as if he wanted badly to believe what Brant was saying. Hiring someone to kill her was one thing. Doing it himself, in cold blood, was quite another. "What do you have in mind?"

"The fact that she's Cletus Brown's daughter should do, for starters," Brant said. He turned and started to pace, the gun hanging at his side. "And I'm sure once we start digging, we'll find all sorts of interesting things we can use."

"It won't work," Austin said. "Even if I believed you'd really help me, she knows too much. She'd make someone listen to her."

His grip eased from Valerie's throat as he turned to watch Brant pace. The gun slipped from her temple just long enough for Valerie to lunge to the floor. Out of the corner of her eye, she saw Austin raise the gun toward her as she rolled for cover.

A shot rang out, barely missing her.

Another shot rang out, and Austin stumbled backward, crashing into her computer as he fell to the floor.

Valerie knew immediately that he was dead. She lifted her gaze to where Brant stood with his weapon still raised. Their eyes met briefly, and then, as if in slow motion, the gun slipped from his hand to the floor.

Without a word, he turned and strode from the room.

AT POLICE HEADQUARTERS, when Valerie was called in to give her statement, Brant avoided her. She saw him in Hugh Rawlins's office, but he barely acknowledged her presence. Instead he got up and strode from the room, leaving an aching silence in his wake.

So that was that, Valerie thought, trying to tell herself it didn't matter. She'd accomplished what she'd set out to do. Her father would soon be a free man. The end justified the means, didn't it?

Apparently not to Brant. His actions made it plain that he would never forgive her for deceiving him.

If he would just give her a chance to explain, she could somehow make him understand.

But he was hurt and embittered by her deception, and Valerie couldn't blame him.

And you put such stock in the truth, he'd once taunted her.

Yes, but only when the truth suited her. Only when the truth didn't complicate her plans.

After she'd given her statement, Captain Rawlins asked her to remain in his office while everyone else left. When they were alone, he said, "I realize what I'm about to ask you is a little unusual, and you can refuse if you want. God knows, you have every right." He closed his eyes briefly, and Valerie realized suddenly how the night's events had affected him, too. He wasn't a Colter, but he was a close family friend. That friendship had been used and betrayed for over thirty years. "Raymond Colter is in custody downstairs. He wants to see you."

Valerie's heart thudded against her chest. "Why?"

Hugh shrugged. "Will you talk to him?"

Talk to the man who had framed her father thirty-one years ago?

Why not? Valerie thought. As a matter of fact, she had a few things she would like to say to him.

VALERIE HAD NEVER MET Raymond Colter, but she would have known him anywhere. He had the same dark hair—sprinkled with gray—and the same dark eyes she'd seen in all the other Colters. But Raymond's eyes were no longer cold with arrogance. His were the eyes of a defeated old man.

He sat at a small wooden table as Valerie was led into

the holding room. He rose when she entered, and for a moment, they gazed at each other silently.

Valerie's throat constricted painfully. Confronting the man who had framed her father wasn't as easy as she'd once thought it would be. Raymond Colter seemed almost pitiful to her now. Almost.

He glanced down at his hands. "I don't expect you to forgive me. I don't expect your father to forgive me, either, but I wanted you to know that it was nothing personal."

Valerie blinked. "Nothing personal?"

"I didn't have anything against Cletus Brown. I didn't even know him. I'd heard about him, though, through his brother-in-law. The two of us got acquainted when I used to moonlight for the Kingsleys. I knew Odell hated Cletus. He would have done anything to get him away from his sister."

Valerie moistened her suddenly dry lips. "You paid him to lie for you."

"I gave him part of the ransom money. Not a lot, but enough to satisfy him."

"Did he help you kidnap Adam?"

Raymond shook his head. "No. It wasn't him. There was this woman named Sally Hoffeinz. She was a widow. Had lost her husband and kid, a little boy, in a car crash. It did something to her. She wasn't right somehow. I dated her a few times—nothing serious on my part—but she got…attached to me. I think she somehow got it twisted in her mind that I was her husband. She would have done anything for me."

"Even help you kidnap a child?" Valerie asked.

"Yeah," Raymond said. "Even that. Only, she went off the deep end when I took the kid. After the ransom drop, I was going to take the boy out into the country somewhere and dump him, you know, where he'd be found in a day or two. But then Sally up and disappeared with him."

Valerie stared at him in shock. "You mean you didn't kill Adam Kingsley?" She wasn't sure if she believed him or not. He was a man fighting for his life, after all.

"As it happened, we were looking for the Tyler kid, too. I had a pretty good idea the stepfather was responsible for the kid's disappearance, so I paid him a little visit. After hours. Convinced him to show me where the body was. I'd taken Adam's pajamas and the blanket from Sally, because I thought the Kingsleys might have to be convinced I had the boy. I put the pajamas on the Tyler kid's body, reasonably certain the Kingsleys would be satisfied the body was Adam's." There was a strange glint in his eyes. Valerie wondered if it was madness. "I knew Iris Kingsley would put pressure on the department to get the body released as quickly as possible, so they could bury the boy and start putting the tragedy behind them. Her son had a political campaign to focus on, and I knew she wouldn't want the distractions prolonged. That was the way she was."

"So you're saying you not only kidnapped a child and framed an innocent man," Valerie said in horror, "but you let a murderer go free."

Raymond's eyes were beginning to glaze over. Valerie wasn't sure how much longer he would remain coherent. "I had to. I knew if Adam's body wasn't found, they'd never stop looking for him. And even if the Kingsleys gave up, Judd wouldn't have. He would have searched the four corners of the earth for that boy. He was the best, after all," Raymond said bitterly.

In that instant, Valerie began to see Judd Colter in a new light. She thought about the night her father had been arrested, the way Judd Colter had treated him. Valerie understood now. Judd Colter had truly believed her father was a kidnapper, a man who had murdered an innocent child; and Judd's rage had been so great, he hadn't been able to contain it.

Given the same evidence, would she have behaved any differently?

Valerie took a deep breath. She let her eyes meet Raymond Colter's for the last time. "Why are you telling me all this?"

"It'll all come out at the trial," he said, then shrugged. "Like I said, I don't expect you to forgive me. But I figured I owed you something."

CHAPTER SIXTEEN

HE'D BEEN IN PRISON for a long time. So long he sometimes lost count of the years. The only thing he knew
for sure was that he would never get out. He'd known
it the day he'd been convicted. The witness that might
have come forward on his behalf had disappeared soon
after he'd been arrested, and the evidence that would
have cleared him had long since been destroyed.

Cletus Brown was past sixty now, an old man. He'd
been locked up for half his life. He could barely remember what his life had been like on the outside; or what
his wife and young daughter had looked like.

Grace would be nearly as old as he if she'd lived,
and little Violet would be in her thirties. Thirty-six, to
be exact. Sometimes it was still hard to believe they
were both gone from his life. There was no one on the
outside who cared about him anymore. No one who even
remembered him. He would die in here, the state would
bury him, and that would be that.

No one would ever know the truth about the night
little Adam Kingsley was kidnapped. Cletus would take
his secrets to the grave with him, not because he wanted
it that way, but because there was no one left who would
listen to him.

He stared out the sealed window of his prison cell and
watched the sunrise—as much of it as he could see. He

closed his eyes and tried to remember what it felt like to have the hot Tennessee sun beating down on his face. But it was no use. His memories had died long ago.

A guard named Tyrell, who had been at the prison almost as long as Cletus, stopped in front of his cell. "You've got a visitor, Cletus. A real looker, they tell me."

Cletus hadn't had a visitor in over fifteen years. Slowly he turned and faced the guard.

"Well, come on," Tyrell urged. "I don't have all day."

Cletus shuffled over to the door and allowed himself to be handcuffed and his ankles shackled. Then the cell door opened and the guard led him to the visitors' area, where he took a seat behind a Plexiglas partition fitted with a small speaker. A young woman in a red suit sat on the other side.

For a moment, Cletus stared at her, speechless. He couldn't believe his eyes. He pressed his shaking hand to the cool glass and tried to blink back the tears that sprang to his eyes.

"Grace?" he whispered, fearing the vision would vanish if he spoke too loudly.

The woman smiled. An angel's smile. Grace's smile. She put her hand up to the glass and pressed it to his. "It's Violet," she said through the speaker. "I've come to take you home, Daddy."

VALERIE SHADED HER EYES against the glaring sun as she walked outside the building and headed across the prison parking lot, toward her car. She wasn't sure if her eyes were stinging from the sun or from unshed tears.

Her father wouldn't be released immediately, she'd

discovered. There was red tape involved, certain proce-
dures that had to be followed, but it was only a formality.
In a few days—weeks at the most—he would be a free
man, and he and Valerie could start a new life together.
Just the two of them.

The tears started again, and Valerie wiped an impatient hand across her face, telling herself it didn't matter
that Brant hadn't called her; hadn't tried to get in touch
with her. He had a lot on his mind. His family was going
through a nightmare right now, and Valerie was a part of
their torment. If she'd never come to town, never started
asking questions—

Her father would have died in prison, she reminded
herself.

She took a deep breath. Maybe it was for the best that
she and Brant go their separate ways. Maybe it was for
the best that they put all this behind them—

She came to an abrupt halt when she looked up and
saw Brant leaning against her car. Then slowly she
started toward him.

"I thought I might find you here." He glanced at the
prison behind her. "Did you see him?"

Valerie nodded, unable to speak.

"I take it the meeting went well."

She struggled with her emotions for a moment, then
said, "He didn't believe me when I told him everything
that had happened. Brant, you should have seen his
face—" She broke off, pressing her fingertips to her
lips. "I'm sorry. I know this is a difficult time for your
family. For you."

She saw the anguish in his eyes and wanted to reach
out to him, but how could she? She was a part of that
anguish.

"You saved my life," she said softly. "He would have killed me."

"I know." Brant gazed down at her. "I'd do the same thing again. Without hesitation. But it doesn't make it any easier to sleep at night."

Valerie nodded in understanding. "I'm sorry I didn't tell you the truth about who I really am. But I couldn't. I didn't think I could—"

"Trust me?"

"You're a Colter," she said miserably.

"Yeah. I'm a Colter." There was something in his voice, something in his eyes, that made Valerie feel so sad for him.

Before she could stop herself, she reached out and placed her hand on his arm. "I was wrong about your father. He was just doing his job. I know that now. He was a good cop, Brant. He cared so much about that little boy."

For the first time, Brant's mood seemed to lighten. "There'll never be another like him. Or so I've been told."

"Oh, I don't know about that," Valerie said. "I can think of one cop who is at least his equal."

His eyes met hers, and this time, the emotion in those dark depths made her heart melt. She bit her lip. "Can you ever forgive me?"

"The question is," he said softly, "can you ever forgive my family? Can you ever forget that I'm a Colter?"

"I don't want to forget," Valerie said. "I like you for who you are. I might even love you," she added, surprising them both.

"Might?" He smiled, and Valerie wanted to shout for joy. It was as if a dark cloud had been lifted from her

world. He took her hand and pulled her against him. She went without the slightest bit of resistance. "That's very interesting," he said. "Because as it happens, I might love you, too."

He kissed her then, in a deep, slow exploration of their growing feelings. After a while, he pulled back and gazed into her eyes. "So, tell me something. Do you think a Yankee girl like you could get used to living in all this heat?"

She smiled. "You're forgetting something. I was born in Memphis. I'm a true Southerner at heart. This is my home, Brant. Now and forever."

"I like the sound of that," he said, before he dipped his head and kissed her again.

Fall in Love with...

MEN
in UNIFORM

YES! Please send me the exciting *Men in Uniform* collection. This collection will begin with 3 FREE BOOKS and 2 FREE GIFTS in my very first shipment—and more valuable free gifts will follow! My books will arrive in 8 monthly shipments until I have the entire 51-book *Men in Uniform* collection. I will receive 2 free books in each shipment and I will pay just $4.49 U.S./$5.39 CDN for each of the other 4 books in each shipment, plus $2.99 for shipping and handling.* If I decide to keep the entire collection, I'll only have paid for 32 books because 19 books are free. I understand that accepting the 3 free books and gifts places me under no obligation to buy anything. I can always return a shipment and cancel at any time. My free books and gifts are mine to keep no matter what I decide.

263 HDK 2653   463 HDK 2653

Name   (PLEASE PRINT)

Address   Apt. #

City   State/Prov.   Zip/Postal Code

Signature (if under 18, a parent or guardian must sign)

Mail to the **Harlequin Reader Service:**
IN U.S.A.: P.O. Box 1867, Buffalo, NY 14240-1867
IN CANADA: P.O. Box 609, Fort Erie, Ontario L2A 5X3

* Terms and prices subject to change without notice. Prices do not include applicable taxes. Sales tax applicable in N.Y. Canadian residents will be charged applicable taxes. This offer is limited to one order per household. All orders subject to approval. Credit or debit balances in a customer's account(s) may be offset by any other outstanding balance owed by or to the customer. Please allow 4–6 weeks for delivery. Offer available while quantities last. Offer not available to Quebec residents.

Your privacy: Harlequin is committed to protecting your privacy. Our Privacy Policy is available online at www.eHarlequin.com or upon request from the Reader Service. From time to time we may make our lists of customers available to reputable third parties who have a product or service of interest to you. If you would prefer we not share your name and address, please check here. ☐

MUBPA10

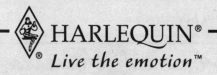

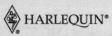

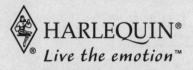

HARLEQUIN®
INTRIGUE®

BREATHTAKING ROMANTIC SUSPENSE

Shared dangers and passions lead to electrifying romance and heart-stopping suspense!

Every month, you'll meet six new heroes who are guaranteed to make your spine tingle and your pulse pound. With them you'll enter into the exciting world of Harlequin Intrigue— where your life is on the line and so is your heart!

THAT'S INTRIGUE— ROMANTIC SUSPENSE AT ITS BEST!

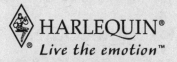

HARLEQUIN®
Presents®

The world's bestselling romance series...
The series that brings you your favorite authors,
month after month:

Helen Bianchin...Emma Darcy
Lynne Graham...Penny Jordan
Miranda Lee...Sandra Marton
Anne Mather...Carole Mortimer
Melanie Milburne...Michelle Reid

and many more talented authors!

Wealthy, powerful, gorgeous men...
Women who have feelings just like your own...
The stories you love, set in exotic, glamorous locations...

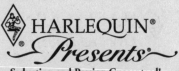

HARLEQUIN®
Presents®

HPDIR08

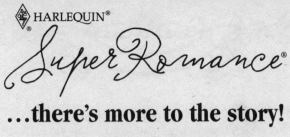

HARLEQUIN®
SuperRomance®

…there's more to the story!

Superromance.
A *big* satisfying read about unforgettable
characters. Each month we offer *six* very different
stories that range from family drama to adventure
and mystery, from highly emotional stories to
romantic comedies—and much more! Stories
about people you'll believe in and care about.
Stories too compelling to put down.…

Our authors are among today's *best* romance
writers. You'll find familiar names and talented
newcomers. Many of them are award winners—
and you'll see why!

If you want the biggest and best
in romance fiction, you'll get it
from Superromance!

Exciting, Emotional, Unexpected…

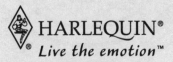

HARLEQUIN®
Live the emotion™

Harlequin® Historical
Historical Romantic Adventure!

Imagine a time of chivalrous knights and unconventional ladies, roguish rakes and impetuous heiresses, rugged cowboys and spirited frontierswomen— these rich and vivid tales will capture your imagination!

Harlequin Historical... they're too good to miss!